SO-EGF-651

A brilliant surgeon . . .
A dazzling medical breakthrough . . .
A deadly international conspiracy
to steal his secret . . . or kill him!

Martha Albrand's

ZURICH AZ900

"A SURE-FIRE TREAT TO SAVOR . . . There's nothing left out: magnificent scenery by way of the Alps, romance brilliantly new and sadly dead, high-powered kidnapping, and, of course, murder . . . Guaranteed to please her legion of fans!"

Boston Herald-Advertiser

"A FIRST-CLASS NOVEL OF SUSPENSE, lifted from the ranks of ordinary thrillers by the uncommon writing talents of Martha Albrand."

New Orleans Times-Picayune

"MISS ALBRAND'S SKILL in characterization, her use of authentic settings and even the homework she has done in medical research not only invite but seduce us into the willing suspension of disbelief."

Los Angeles Times

Other Avon Books by
Martha Albrand

AFTER MIDNIGHT	14985	$ .95
DAY IN MONTE CARLO	04168	$ .75
DESPERATE MOMENT	17079	$ .95
ENDURE NO LONGER	17467	$1.25
HUNTED WOMAN	04176	$ .75
LINDEN AFFAIR	15230	$ .95
MANHATTAN NORTH	04663	$ .75
MASK OF ALEXANDER	15883	$ .95
MEET ME TONIGHT	04226	$ .75
NIGHTMARE IN COPENHAGEN	15487	$ .75
NO SURRENDER	04366	$ .75
NONE SHALL KNOW	14274	$ .75
OBSESSION OF EMMET BOOTH	18010	$ .95
REMEMBERED ANGER	14464	$ .75
RHINE REPLICA	04499	$ .75
WAIT FOR THE DAWN	14696	$ .95
WHISPERING HILL	04200	$ .75
WITHOUT ORDERS	04465	$ .75

MARTHA ALBRAND
ZURICH AZ900

AVON
PUBLISHERS OF BARD, CAMELOT, DISCUS, EQUINOX AND FLARE BOOKS

All the persons and events in this book are entirely imaginary; nothing in it derives from anything that ever happened.

AVON BOOKS
A division of
The Hearst Corporation
959 Eighth Avenue
New York, New York 10019

Copyright © 1974 by Martha Albrand.
Published by arrangement with Holt, Rinehart and Winston, Inc.
Library of Congress Catalog Card Number: 73-16862

All rights reserved, which includes the right
to reproduce this book or portions thereof in
any form whatsoever. For information address
Holt, Rinehart and Winston, Inc.,
383 Madison Avenue, New York, New York 10017.

ISBN: 0-380-00469-0

First Avon Printing, September, 1975.

AVON TRADEMARK REG. U.S. PAT. OFF. AND
FOREIGN COUNTRIES, REGISTERED TRADEMARK—
MARCA REGISTRADA, HECHO EN CHICAGO, U.S.A.

Printed in the U.S.A.

To F. M.

I am grateful to Dr. Gene Schwartz for medical advice and to Catherine Hutter for her encouragement and help.

1

"We will meet you at the Kunsthaus at twelve-thirty sharp. Under Monet's *Man with the Sun Umbrella*."

The voice came over the wire, high-pitched and angry. Graham Foley recoiled. He did not look forward to direct contact with his employer. But at least the man had picked a painting he loved. It made him think back, for a moment, to the time when he had hoped to become an artist, before his family had lost their money and he'd had to go to work, mundane work. No more art courses. But he still painted, for relaxation. Sentimental scenes—sunsets, seascapes, children at play. He had sold his work only once, to the man who had introduced him to his present employer. He had bought three. For a good price. Graham Foley hadn't realized at the time that it was part of the plan.

Undercover agents, he thought, loath to call what he was doing by its correct name, always met at stations, cemeteries, zoos, museums, and usually at a time when most civilized people were lunching. In Switzerland—in Paris too—some men still went home for lunch and took a nap afterwards. Solid traditions. Others had the normal business date in a restaurant. But with people like him, nothing proceeded normally.

He was at the Kunsthaus a little ahead of time. Perhaps the museum would raise his spirits. The dramatic structural composition at the entrance—red, purple, and blue mesh streamers spanned on bright yellow wiring, like transparent sails as high as the building itself—was not exactly restorative, but it did serve to distract one, and he was grateful for that.

Punctually at twelve-thirty, he was waiting on the wide balustrade under the Monet painting, standing with a non-chalance he wasn't feeling at all. Yes, he liked the picture. It could have been modern. The man's blue trousers looked like jeans, and the effeminate way he carried an umbrella against the sun. . . . He heard the clatter of crutches, and froze. Then he pulled himself together and joined his employer.

"That black and white dog . . . is it supposed to be a Dalmatian?"

"Could be," said Graham. "Or just a mutt."

Impossible to describe the man's face, something like a lump of clay into which a child had poked two dents for the eyes, something that was supposed to pass for a nose, no bridge, just two rather disgusting holes, and a thin line for the mouth. Just as impossible to tell his age. Forty, fifty; younger, older? You got lost wondering about the large ears running from his balding head almost to his mouth. And the voice! As if the vocal cords had been damaged. Maybe they had been. Still, it was impossible to feel pity for the man. Graham knew almost nothing about him, not his address, not his telephone number, and his name was surely assumed. Smith. P. Smith. Schmitt, sometimes; or Schmidt. Graham didn't even know the man's nationality. Face, voice, speech—they betrayed nothing. All he knew was the unlisted number through which the man could be reached.

"I'm afraid we're going to have to use someone else."

The imperial "we" always irritated Graham. "Why, sir?"

"You're not getting anywhere."

"I've done my best." Graham Foley's face was red with anger and he was aware that his voice was almost as strident as Smith's, which only increased his rage. "I've bugged his girl's apartment, but they don't talk about it. I got into his office at the Kantonspital, and that was no simple matter. I went through every file case—nothing. I understand he also works on it at home."

"So?"

10

"I'm getting around to that next. But it's not the sort of thing that can be done overnight."

"Not overnight, but you've had more than a month."

Foley had turned his back on the Monet and was staring down at the agonized Rodin *Orpheus* in the center of the room. "I think, if you'll permit my saying so, sir, aren't you perhaps going after this thing prematurely? He doesn't seem to consider it ready . . ."

"You fool!" said the man. "We'd be dead by now if it weren't for him, and you damn well know it."

Foley damn well did know that some time ago the famous Swiss cardiovascular surgeon, Anton Zeller, had tried out a vaccine on Smith, something he had been developing for years. He had to admire Smith, Schmitt, Schmidt, for his readiness to act as guinea pig. It had taken guts. And it had paid off. Atherosclerosis would have closed in; by this time Smith would have been paralyzed by a stroke, or senile. The restoration of his faculties, according to what Graham had been told, was nothing short of a miracle. A pity, he thought, that they hadn't left the man to rot.

"I checked his farm in Maur. He's got a bloody zoo there. He's built on the place where he has his animals slaughtered. I talked to the butcher who works for him. All he knows is that Zeller uses some parts of calves, freshly slaughtered calves—that seems to be important—but he didn't know what parts. By the way, did you know the Swiss reservists are allowed to keep their rifles at home? Think what would happen in some countries if every . . ."

"Stick to the point. You weren't successful there either?"

"I almost got shot trying to get into the lab."

"Well, see that you do better with whatever you're working on now. You've got two more weeks. No results by then, and you're fired." With that Smith worked his way down the three steps and out of the room with unbelievable speed.

For a good five minutes Graham Foley didn't move. To be fired from this job meant elimination.

2

The whirr of a helicopter.

Anton Zeller stopped short, listening to the dying sound of the motor. The aircraft had been announced a good hour earlier; somewhere it must have run into trouble. In the mountains, probably, where it had picked up a patient. A possible amputee. It wasn't his concern, Professor Buerkli would take care of the man. Still, he waited until he heard the barely audible thump with which the machine landed on the pad of Floor F.

There weren't many hospitals to which people in need of immediate help could be flown directly, to the very source of professional aid. He remembered others where it took time that could be fatal, endless minutes before the ambulances from outlying airports, hindered by traffic or fog, their sirens wailing, could reach vitally needed aid. You could say what you liked against Switzerland, but not that this small country didn't offer the most modern of medical services.

God, he needed a cup of coffee. Satisfaction, the relief of satisfaction, could deflate you just as profoundly as failure. Besides, it had been a hard day. The bypass had been routine, but the last operation, involving mitral and aortic valves at the same time, had taken a lot out of him.

Instead of going directly to the elevator, he stopped at the nurses' station. Buerkli was certainly one of the ablest surgeons in his field, but sometimes he liked to confer with Zeller. Nobody in the room but Sister Clara. She gave him

12

a look that said clearly, "You think the department can't live without you, don't you?"

Sister Clara had never liked him. And there were others who felt as she did. Anton Zeller, chief of cardiovascular surgery, didn't fit in with their idea of a serious and important personality. It was partly the way he dressed, informally—blue jeans and open shirt in summer, the same in the winter, except that the jeans were of heavier material, the shirt a light wool. And he wore a jacket of well-worn leather. His sandals were expensive Guccis, yet to the average middle-class citizen they were plain hippie wear. Then there were those who found him arrogant and haughty. He was neither. He knew he didn't possess De-Bakey's infallibility and magical stamina, or Ted Diethrich's incredibly fast hands, but he was good. Very good, in fact, and proud of it. Others objected to the fact that he drove a Cadillac, a new one every year, all of them guzzling gasoline as wild Irishmen down beer, but he enjoyed the concentration and skill it took to maneuver the wide car through Zurich's narrow, winding streets. Once, hurtling down the steep gradient of the Krönleinstrasse, his actual speed seemingly accelerated by the closeness of the villas on either side, Helene's brother, accustomed to the wide, open highways of Texas, had clutched the edge of his seat, his eyes open wide, and muttered, "Man, don't you ever blow your horn on these curves?" Hank had crashed and burned to death a few years later in one of his Jaguars, on a wide, open highway of Texas.

Zeller left his message for Buerkli with Sister Clara, who responded unintelligibly. Her resentment of him, however, had nothing to do with his appearance or the way he drove, but was based on personal feelings—he had never paid her the attention she felt was her due as one of the most competent nurses in the hospital. As a woman she could hardly have expected attention, she was painfully plain; yet apparently this was part of it too, as evidenced in her treatment of the prettier nurses.

And then there was Lisa.

Lisa. It was her day off, and he'd not only had to cancel their meeting for lunch, he hadn't even called to tell her he'd be too late to take her out for dinner at seven. He hesitated. Should he phone? But seeing every booth occupied, he decided it would only delay him further. In the small lounge where the vending machines stood, a few orderlies were playing cards. He decided not to stop for coffee either.

He shed his white coat on one of the racks in the cloakroom next to the exit that led to the parking lot reserved for doctors. Suddenly he grinned, a boyish grin. Those who liked him found it lovable; those who didn't found it calculating. What had brought it on was the sudden memory of Houston Methodist where he had spent almost eight years working under DeBakey in the subspecialty which had always been his ambition—cardiovascular surgery. Here, in the hospital parking lot, there were no gypsies, as there had been during an unforgettable period in Houston. They had thought nothing of squatting on the roof of someone's car, to sleep or eat, or to just sit palavering endlessly as to whether or not they should pay for the medical services rendered to a sick member of their tribe, should he or she die. They would refuse to move, and often it took long discussions before one could repossess one's car. Certainly patients in the Kantonspital crowded the corridors when the small waiting rooms were filled to capacity, and would pile up in front of the treatment rooms, but at Methodist the gypsies had taken over every available space, bedding down for the night, making the waiting rooms and corridors their temporary home. The grin faded as he recalled how nobody, not even DeBakey, had paid much attention to him at first, and he had felt useless, depressed, and somehow offended. That had been in the early sixties, when euphoria had raged and doctors still believed in heart transplants. He had been thirty. Now he was forty-one.

He got into his car and drove past the high-rise nurses' home, the university complex, the Eidgenössische Technische Hochschule, to the Winterthuererstrasse where Lisa lived.

3

Lisa Tanner walked restlessly through her apartment. Usually she took pride in the small one-and-a-half rooms she could at last call her own. For a couple of years she had lived in the Schwesternhochhaus, opposite the Kantonspital. Although most of the nurses each had her own room in the tall building, often they had to share bath and kitchen—a constant source of petty quarrels over someone using somebody else's pan, or towel, or breaking open a new bottle of cleaning stuff when the old one wasn't quite empty. Besides, it was hardly entertaining to spend one's free time in the same company with those one saw constantly while on duty. Endless gossip about each other, patients, and doctors.

Before that she had lived near the university with a family who rented furnished rooms. The bathtub had stood in the kitchen on four legs, shedding paint because of the heat from the stove. It had been almost impossible to know when to take a bath. Somebody was always sitting in the tub, or was cooking or eating. She had been lucky to find complete privacy finally, even if it meant climbing two rather steep flights and rising early to catch the streetcar.

Her restlessness wasn't caused by Zeller's being late; he had been late many times before. Nor was she hurt by the fact that he had had to cancel their lunch. She was used to that, too, and respected his excuses which invariably were connected with his work. Her restlessness was rooted in

15

her decision, a decision it had taken her nearly half a year to reach. If . . . she thought . . . if only he . . . and heard the key in the lock.

The moment she saw him, her mood changed. He looked so tired, all she could feel was pity. She took the small overnight bag he always carried in the back of his car, with its clean white shirt and blue suit, and put it down on a chair. She pointed to the couch. "Sit down. Stretch out."

"Just let me catch my breath. Then I'll shower and change."

"We don't have to go out. We can eat here."

The words came fast, before she had reflected on what she was saying.

"But you're all dressed up."

"Doesn't matter."

"And you went to a lot of trouble. I can see. You look beautiful."

Actually he had never thought of her as beautiful, and she wasn't. She was more than that. As a patient had described her once, she wore her soul on her face. Alive, warm, sympathetic to almost anything with which she came in touch—people, animals, nature, even inanimate things. No matter what she wore, dressed up or plain, he would always see her the way he had seen her first, when he had literally stumbled over her. Worried suddenly about a postoperative heart case, he had gone back to the hospital to check. He had glanced at the monitor in the coronary care unit, then opened the door to his patient's room, and there she was, on the floor, a blanket wrapped into a roll under her head, another covering her partially, one slender leg in white knee socks sticking out from under. The knee was round and tanned. Her hair, spilling freely over the rolled blanket, was the color that had always delighted him as a boy, when he had peeled the prickly shell from the young chestnuts on which he used to carve designs. At first he thought she was a visitor, a worried relative who had managed to sneak in. Then, when she sat up, he saw her uniform and the Red Cross brooch.

"Where is Sister Mari?"

He had asked for the stern Finnish nurse, one of their

16

best. He looked at the monitor over the patient's bed. Okay, so far.

"She seemed to be coming down with a cold and we thought it best to avoid any chance of infection. She gave me your instructions. They've been followed accurately." She passed him the sheet of the last three hours. He glanced at it, then checked the man.

"And who are you?"

"Schwester Lisa."

"Never saw you before."

It was rude, but she smiled. The smile made her eyes shine. Like her hair, they were chestnut colored. "I've only been here a month."

"Fresh from the Red Cross?"

"No. I've worked with them for two years since my training."

"Instructions remain the same. Should there be any change, call the resident first, then have him contact me. Good night."

"Good night." But she wasn't looking at him, as most nurses did when they met him for the first time. She was adjusting the patient's arm and hand into which the intravenous drip was flowing from the bottle above his head. He walked out into the monitoring room. The nurse on duty knew what was coming. Her voice a mixture of justification and apology, she told him before he could speak, "We had no choice, Herr Professor. That's why Dr. Walter thought it wasn't necessary to notify you. She volunteered, after having worked all day. She's very good."

"A sleepy nurse . . ."

"She won't go to sleep, not with all the coffee she's had. Besides, she took some Dexedrine to make sure she'd stay awake."

"She was on the floor when I came."

"Anything wrong with stretching out when your back aches?"

These Yugoslavs were impossible. They always had an answer and it usually made sense. "When your back aches it isn't easy to jump up."

"She'll jump up. She's like a deer, fast and noiseless."

A deer. Yes. Anton Zeller looked at Lisa with a smile

17

that was almost carefree. Within half a year she had become his favorite surgical nurse.

"Fix me a martini."

One of his habits brought home from the United States. She didn't care for mixed drinks. "Look what I was given today," she said, coming back from the kitchen, holding up a bottle of champagne. "Moët. Bless grateful patients. But you've got to open it. I can't get the wire off. And don't shoot at my favorite picture."

"You shouldn't waste it on me." He took the napkin she handed him.

"Why not? I'm certainly not going to drink it alone." Besides, she thought, the champagne might help her.

He eased the cork out gently. A soft fizzle as the imprisoned bubbles escaped. He poured their glasses full, tossed down his without toasting her, then poured himself a second. "To you." And a third. Then the alcohol hit him. He leaned back, closed his eyes. "For just a moment." But an hour passed before he awoke, stretched. "I needed that."

She had covered him with a throw. He pushed it aside. Where was she?

"Lisa."

"Coming."

She had changed into slacks. She was bearing a caquelon on a tray which she set down on a card table with a white cloth. "Fondue. Everything's ready."

She had an instinct for gauging time, the time a man needed to rest, the time when pain would set in, the time not to disturb. It was what made her such a good nurse. She had a glass of water ready before the patient asked for it; she never had to be told to please raise or lower the bed or rearrange pillows.

"Fresh strawberries, whipped cream, and if the champagne's gone stale, I can open the bottle of wine you brought last week."

The little white squares of bread had been kept warm in a heating basket. They dunked their long forks into the thick yellow dip, drinking kirsch instead of wine. "Want to talk?" she asked.

"About today? Not yet."

Suddenly there was a frown between his brows, so deep

18

it seemed to split his forehead. She knew he had operated that afternoon on a patient he had been treating for more than three months with his new suspension. "How did Regina do?"

"All right."

Better than all right, Lisa knew. Regina, who took her place when Zeller operated on her day off, was one of the most experienced OR nurses at the hospital. "Just tell me how it went."

"Practically no obstruction in the lumen of the arteries, or, if you like, a considerable reduction of the fatty plaque areas when compared with the last angiogram." The frown was gone; elation colored his voice.

She shared it with him. Since she had become his surgical nurse two years ago, she had lived with his fanatic pursuit of something that would at least arrest, if not cure, the inexorable, disastrous progression of atherosclerosis. The man he had operated on was serving a life sentence in Regensdorf. After an arteriogram had disclosed an advanced stage of occlusion in the aorta, the man had volunteered for the experimental treatment, even after its possible hazards had been explained to him. Evidently the man's courage had been rewarded. For Zeller the results were a great encouragement.

"I wonder if it comforts him," she said, "to know that even though imprisoned, he still has been able to do something for mankind."

Zeller shook his head, smiling. "Oh, my romantic Lisa. What on God's earth could compensate a man for the loss of his freedom?"

She began to clear the dishes, almost noiselessly so as not to disturb his thoughts. She even managed to close the card table without making a sound. He had always admired her way of moving quietly, like a shadow in a dream. It calmed him. Without any of his usual impatience he said, "I'm going to try it next on a fairly young fellow, also in Regensdorf. At thirty-eight he didn't believe his arteries could be hardening. But when he heard how well my patient was doing . . . he's been pestering the authorities ever since. So I've scheduled him to start next week." His face was serious again.

"Does this mean that AZ 900 is ready for synthetic mass production?"

"Hardly," he said curtly.

He had named the result of his research AZ 900 without the slightest modesty about using his initials for an invention that might make medical history.

"So when will it be safe?"

"When I say so."

"And poor Enrico will have to go on waiting."

"Poor Enrico is much better at waiting than you are. He understands me perfectly. Never any kind of pressure."

"That's because he's such a wonderful man."

"Is that so?" His tone was teasing. "You hardly know him."

"I don't have to. It shines out of his face. A good man. And such a devoted father and husband. Maybe I'm in a hurry for you two to start producing it because I want to see him successful. He's the kind to whom money means only what he can do for his family. I suppose that's the Italian in him."

"I am beginning to feel jealous of Enrico, perfect husband and father," said Zeller, with mock seriousness. "Come here," and he opened his arms wide, like a swan spreading his wings to gather in his endangered brood. He pulled her down to him on the couch. She smelled as only Lisa could smell—clean, fresh, with just a touch of an unknown spice. His lips closed on her delicate mouth, delicate in spite of its generous wideness. "Get undressed, girl. Let's not waste any more time."

"Are you staying here or going home afterward?"

"Going home."

Lisa rose. "Then you'd better go right now."

He stared at her, taken aback by the tone of her voice, his ice blue eyes turning the color of Alpine snow at dusk. "What does that mean?"

"You know what it means."

Her change of attitude struck him like an unpredicted storm, the last thing he could have expected from a sky so serene a minute before. For a moment he hated her for interrupting his feeling of well-being just when he at last felt able to relax. And to him, relaxation meant sex.

"You've lost your sense of timing."

"Sorry." She sat up straight. "But I can't go on like this."

"Like what?"

"You know very well."

"Don't be ridiculous."

"I am not being ridiculous."

"Thousands of people live together without being married."

"And I would, if you didn't have a wife."

"I said I'd get a divorce. And I've tried. As you know."

And with no result, she thought. How hard had he really tried?

"It isn't easy to have an affair with a man who has the position you have. It's not that I feel embarrassed when I walk into the hospital with all eyes on me, or when your colleagues pinch my fanny because they wonder what you've got that they don't have. And it's not because it's like living on a way station. It's this damn thing that every time we make love and I want to turn and put my head on the shoulder of the man who's made me happy, he's gone. He's in somebody else's bed and I'm lying alone. I know men feel differently about it. They've had what they wanted, so after that . . ."

"I never thought of you as just a good lay."

This was ugly and she almost got up, then controlled herself. It was probably her fault. She shouldn't have chosen an evening when he was so exhausted to spring her decision on him, but now it was too late.

"You gave up Chris for me. Why don't you say it?"

"I gave up Chris because I fell in love with you. But Chris wants children."

"I'll give you a child."

"I don't want an illegitimate child."

"You sound like the nineteenth century. I thought you were more sophisticated."

"Then you were wrong. I want a normal home, which means a husband and a father for my children. And I don't want them raised under female influence alone, jealous of children who have two parents. And I don't want to have to stand up for something I don't believe in."

"Just because your father walked out on you when you were six . . ."

Her face went blank. She could have struck him, but she answered quietly, "That's right. I know what it means, and that's probably why I feel so strongly about it."

Her father, Zeller knew, had been a vineyard worker before he had been dismissed for drunkenness, after which he had decamped, leaving a wife who had been too proud to try to trace him.

"I'd rather have had him," said Lisa, "whatever he was, than grow up without a man in the house."

"You're only twenty-five. You can wait a while longer."

"Until children are a chore?" She shook her head. "No."

She had never made a scene before. And now a thought struck him and, to his surprise, upset him. "Seeing Chris again?"

"Yes."

"He still wants to marry you?"

"Yes."

"You'd be bored stiff."

"That's not the worst thing in life."

"Oh, but it is."

He could see the young assistant to the American consulate in Zurich, tall and lean like himself, typically Harvard Law, typically American. A man who would help clear up after supper, stack the dishwasher, carry the laundry to the laundromat, and cook an edible meal when necessary. Raised in the American tradition of honoring his family above everything else, ready to overlook a little one-shot affair, but believing firmly in faithfulness and the duties of a father as head of the family. A man who, in spite of his youth, had no understanding for the many changing values all over the world.

"Are you really so unhappy?"

It was, Lisa thought, the first civilized question since she had started to reveal what was on her mind. "Terribly."

"Don't you know that I love you?"

"To a certain extent."

"Meaning what?"

"Oh, darling, don't you know yourself? Don't you know

that you draw the line the moment anything interferes with your convenience?"

Because what she said was true, it angered him. He couldn't deny the fact that what he cared about most was time, time unencumbered, time to pursue his profession, his research, his absorbed way of life. Lisa was comfortable, and in her quiet way exciting. At once calming and elating, she shared above all a deep understanding of the importance of his aims. But she had more than empathy, she had passion. He threw off his jacket. "Let's skip it for now. This is a waste of time. I'll marry you and make you a dozen children." He pulled up his shirt.

"No."

"Stop being foolish."

"I wish I could."

She was close to tears—he knew by the way she bit her lower lip, though actually he had never seen her cry. "It's simply that I can't stand it any longer."

"Stand what?"

"Your leaving me after we've made love."

"What else?"

"Oh . . . lots of things."

"Like what?"

"I told you. I want to have children. I want a man I can call my own. I want a man who doesn't have to write me letters or leave me notes, however sweetly written, to remind me of his love. But all that's the least of it. I need more than just passion and a wonderful climax. *I need to belong.*"

He made for the bathroom, the upper part of his body naked, tanned. She stopped him. "No, Toni. Go home. Or stay. You know, we've never stayed a whole night together. Not once. And when you leave me, I lie there crying. I know you think I am contented, but actually I'm feeling cheap and lonely."

"What do you want? Do I have to give it to you in writing that I'll marry you as soon as I can?"

"I don't want anything of the sort," she said, so calmly it alarmed him. "I just want to call it quits. I can't be the other woman in your life any longer."

"Lisa!" It came out loud, as if he were trying to shout

her to her senses. "What more can I do than promise you everything you want?"

"Keep your promises," she said, in that same quiet tone. "But I don't think you can. I know now that it's not a question of divorcing Helene, but the time it would take—time spent with lawyers, time spent in court, time you want for other things—the time you can't spare because your work is more important to you."

"Not just to me. All men feel the same way."

"Not all men."

"All right. Marry your mediocre Chris, who has nothing better to do than file papers and play second fiddle at consular functions." He picked up his shirt and put it on, then picked up his jacket and slung it over his shoulder. His hands were shaking. He hoped she wouldn't notice it. "Good luck."

"Thanks," she said, and then, "my God, what has happened to us?"

She began to cry, her face crumpling like a child's, her mouth squaring. "It's the first time I've seen you look ugly."

He took her in his arms and held her close. She was trembling. "I'll stay tonight." But she shook her head. "It's not just tonight, don't you understand? It's every night. Go now, please. And don't come back unless you really have the time for me I need."

For a moment he stood undecided. He hated crying women, but her tears touched him, the first he had ever seen from her. As always, when he was embarrassed or moved, words failed him. "Now, now, darling . . ."

"Go," she said. "Toni, go."

He still couldn't believe she meant it. He realized that he had thought she was acting in an overemotional moment. But she repeated what she had said, in the same clear incisive tone, and after a few minutes he started to go. At the entrance, he turned, but she was no longer there. Quietly, as usual, she had vanished. The roses he had sent her at the beginning of the week were still fresh, open wide, their yellow centers making them look like wild flowers. She had a way with flowers. They seemed to last forever.

"Lisa."

But there was no answer. He opened the entrance door, held it for a few seconds, called out her name again, and when still there was no response he slammed the door so hard the roses trembled long after he was gone.

4

He drove like a wild man. The new autolane on the Forchstrasse made nothing of the twenty-five-minute drive to Maur, the small village just beyond which he owned a farm. Here and there apartment houses, symmetrically windowed cement structures, intruded into a countryside that had once been undulating field and vineyard in every shade of green. Construction cranes, cheerfully painted bright yellow or red, cut right angles into the sky, evidence of still another building going up to accommodate the thousands yearning to get away from the city, here as everywhere. Car owners now, they didn't mind driving to work into Zurich.

He left the highway and drove a short way on a road that wound through woods. The small village of Maur held little attraction for city people. The local inn was frequented mostly by peasants who met there to play *jass,* a popular Swiss card game, and to drink their red wine. He turned left on a small dirt road that led up a hill to his farm. The place was surrounded by an electrified barbed-wire fence intended to keep the animals within from straying and to make it more difficult for outsiders to trespass, for it was a fact that his "zoo," as the natives exaggeratedly called it, had aroused a lot of irritating curiosity.

He had bought the farm a few years ago when he had known at last just what he was after. Already as a medical student, during his first autopsies, and even more in later heart surgery, he had been struck to see the havoc wrought by fatty plaques in the arteries of comparatively young people suffering from atherosclerosis, a disease that until recently had been considered limited to the aged. Yet not a vestige of such plaques in humans under twenty, or in babies. There was a substance—still elusive, still unidentified—found in the innermost layer of the blood vessels, the intima, of babies, even of teenagers, which evidently prevented the deposit of the menacing fatty substance. Couldn't the answer lie here? Or in the active thymus gland of the very young, which degenerated into fat after human growth was concluded. The thymus could be excised, one could experiment with it, taking it from young animals. His conclusions had been that simple. Less simple had been the years of trial and failure.

The electronic eye on his car opened the gate, his headlights tearing holes of light into the dark night. The dogs gave alarm. By the time he had reached the open space in front of the house, the two men who took care of the livestock were already standing, rifles in hand, next to the huge linden tree encircled by a primitive bench.

Zeller felt foolish. "It's only me," he said. "Everything all right?"

Casper spoke up. "Everything is fine."

"So, nothing since last week." On Friday, someone had broken open one of the hutches where Zeller kept the rabbits he had been feeding on a high-cholesterol diet. The intruder had even tried to get into the house, but by then Casper had heard him.

"Didn't the dogs raise hell?" Zeller had asked.

"No. Our poachers are getting more up-to-date. The dogs were tranquilized with darts."

Zeller had frowned. "Somebody's been watching too much television. Maybe we should put better locks on the lab."

He glanced now at the row of hutches, at the big barn where the cows were kept. It hid the shed where he housed his monkeys, the most important animal for his experiments.

"I'll need a calf next week," he told the man. "Do we have to buy one or is there one ready?" And would Lisa still be willing to assist him, he wondered.

"There are three available."

"Fine. Sorry to have disturbed you. Good night."

He turned the car around. It had begun to rain softly. A policeman in blue-gray uniform with the belt drawn tight and the Zurich crest on his left breast pocket, stopped him. "You're speeding." But when Zeller turned on the lights inside the car, the officer recognized him. "Oh, it's you, Herr Professor. Emergency?"

"Yes."

"I see. But take it easy or you might have a second one."

"Thanks."

They saluted each other, Zeller with a V sign, the officer with his white-gloved hand to the visor of his military cap. Zeller heeded the man's advice. No use getting himself killed or hitting someone.

He reached his home on the Zurichberg. Quite a few condominiums had been rammed in between the older villas on the hill, and he had finally bought one of the former because Helene had hated the old house in the city which he had inherited. "At least here we have a view," she had said, when they had made the move. "It's crazy to live in Switzerland and not have a view."

Their apartment on the steep, winding Krönleinstrasse, almost a chasm between the stone walls and high bushes of the houses on either side, looked down on Lake Zurich and the mountains beyond. When there was *Föhn* you could see the inner Schwyz, the Rigi, Vrenli's Gärtli, the Albis. Helene said she found the sight of the mountains uplifting; she liked the shopping area so close. All she had to do was walk a straight narrow path downhill to get whatever she wanted. And it was quieter than the house in the city which he would always miss, one of the last patrician buildings on the Stockerstrasse to remain uncommercialized. No posters desecrated its gray stone façade, no insurance company had bought it and turned it into an office building—yet. The geraniums still spilled, thick as a cushion, over its wrought-iron balcony. Down the street stood the brick-and-stone block-size Rothschild Palace, which he remembered as it was before doctors and lawyers had filled it with offices. Fetters of a happy childhood that he should have shaken off long ago.

He drove into the garage, then took the elevator up.

He walked into their bedroom and thought how odd it was that Helene had insisted on sleeping in the same room with him when he had wanted to use the guest room for himself. She was fast asleep. He hadn't intended to disturb her, but the speed with which he had driven was still with him. The drive hadn't calmed the complex feelings Lisa had aroused.

He switched on the light. Asleep she didn't look pretty, but then only children did, or adults who hadn't grown up. But even awake she wasn't what one would call a pretty woman. Always too heavy, and now with a premature spread of the hips. Her square face wasn't attractive, although her features were finely chiseled when taken one by one, as if some artist had chosen to create one face on top of another. Yet, as always, she looked like a perfect lady. White nightgown with long sleeves, uncreased even after she'd slept in it, the small lace collar tied with a neat bow. She was lying very straight in her bed, next to his, her hands folded across her chest. Nicely embalmed, he couldn't help thinking. On the bedside table there was an open book, about something called transactional analysis. She had urged him to read it. She had stuck with psychology, majored in it, written a quite decent thesis on Jung. Probably why she could put up with him.

"Helene."

She didn't stir. Lately she had taken to sleeping pills. He shook her awake. "Helene."

She opened her eyes sleepily. "What is it?"

"Me. Anton."

She glanced at the alarm clock. "Two o'clock." Her voice was thick. "Why did you wake me?"

"I want to talk to you."

"Now? For God's sake . . ."

"Now."

"Can't it wait?"

"No. I've already waited too long. I can't wait any longer."

"May I know to what you're referring?" Her voice was clearing and, as always, was immaculately, coolly polite. Politeness, under all circumstances, was her basic approach to life. It didn't cost anything but control, it kept one out of trouble, and it could serve as a weapon.

He sat down in an old-fashioned rocking chair, a nursing chair on short legs that she'd brought with her. It was the only thing from home that she'd wanted. "About two years ago I asked you for a divorce," he said, rocking gently back and forth.

"I said no."

"You did. But I never really found out why."

"Because I thought you would get over her. You have gotten over so many."

"Don't exaggerate. There weren't that many. Anyhow, I'm asking you again."

She looked at him with eyes that bulged slightly, was silent, keeping him waiting, enjoying it. When she finally answered, her tone hadn't changed. "The answer is still no."

"Why? You don't love me."

"Love?" She reached for a cigarette. Cigarettes were her lifeline. She clung to them whenever she felt tense or nervous, which was practically always. "It's hard to love a man like you."

"Why?"

"You're so self-sufficient. It makes one feel superfluous. Although I did love you at first because you were a good lover."

They hadn't slept together for years, but when he had married her it had been a challenge to make this proud, cold creature moan with delight. And during these years he was certain she had never had another man. It was against her code: married women simply didn't find satisfaction anywhere else but with their husbands.

"Why no?" he asked. "When there's nothing we share, nothing we enjoy together. Not even each other's company."

"We share something." She blew a small cloud of smoke between them. It made him cough. "Convenience. I think that's what you'd call it. We don't get in each other's way."

"That's not enough. Not by far. There's more to life than that. Certainly *I'm* not prepared to settle for anything so dreary. And you didn't even want a child from me. You had an abortion without telling me."

"Because even by the wildest stretch of the imagination,

I couldn't see you as a good father. Lisa, I take it, wants children."

"So do I."

"Since when?"

"Since now."

"Your bad luck." She lit another cigarette from the stub of the first. "I'm too old to have any, and I hope the girl has the good sense not to mess up her life with an illegitimate one."

"She wouldn't care."

"She wouldn't? Don't be a fool."

He had no intention of drawing Lisa into the conversation. "Even if she didn't exist, I'd want a divorce."

"I said no," she replied, "and that's it."

Whatever had made him marry her? Right now he couldn't think of a reason. Then a scene came back to him. A sunny Sunday afternoon when "the American girl" had gone sailing with him. Rapperswil and the small hotel where they served such delicious blue trout. He had spoken about his problems, how he had to find the best teacher in the world to study the subspecialty that was his ambition, cardiovascular surgery. "DeBakey. Cooney. If I could get to one of them . . ."

"Send them your last paper. I'm sure one or the other would be impressed." And then, finishing her trout, with a blob of butter glistening on her full lips, saying it casually, "My father gave a lot of money to Houston Methodist."

He had looked at her with a different interest, but said nothing. No doubt about it, her connections had helped.

When had they met? Memory eluded him. At the university, here in Zurich? At some social occasion? Or both. She was older than he, by two or three years, already postgraduate before he'd begun his surgical training. It hadn't seemed important. "The fat girl isn't bad," one of the students had told him, "and she's rich." Money, however, had never played a part in it. He was financially independent, always had been, even more so when his widowed mother had left him their small, secure family fortune. So at least as far as money was concerned he owed her no debt of gratitude. And he could have gone to Paris, or to Philadelphia. There were other heart surgeons to whom he would have had an in through personal connections of his own, or of his professors. But she had held out for Houston. She wanted to show him off at home. Apparently she hadn't had all that many men to show off, in spite of her wealth, perhaps because that was the one thing everyone in her set had. Or perhaps because in her own milieu they'd known her long enough to size her up as the bitch she was.

"But you're not happy with me," he said helplessly.

"Happy?" She drew out the word. "Happiness is for children. Maturity arrives at contentment."

"So you're content."

"As far as is humanly possible—yes."

He knew that her contentment rested in the knowledge that she was the wife of a successful man: content with a beautiful home which she kept immaculate and redecorated constantly, something that puzzled her conservative Swiss friends, friends who probably commiserated with her for his lack of time and his escapades with pretty girls; content with a clique who gossiped about her nastily behind her back. She was proud to be his wife, proud that her confidence in him had proved right.

"Still—and I repeat—I want a divorce."

"To marry Lisa?"

He had never been able to lie. "Eventually."

"No," she said. "Never."

"Did you say never?"

"You heard me."

Nothing in his face showed how dejected he was, how close to despair. He had always kept his needs to himself. Helene had no idea how deeply he needed a woman's absolute devotion. And Lisa had meant what she said; he knew he couldn't sway her.

He got up and went over to Helene. By the look in her eyes he could see she was afraid of him, but she didn't move. She inhaled and again blew out some blue smoke, but this time in little curls that floated around her in rings until, ever widening, they dissolved like clouds in a light wind.

"You won't give me up," he said, "because you don't want to see me happy."

"Probably."

"Then you don't leave me any choice."

32

He walked into their dressing room. On shelves above his clothes lay his luggage. He packed a small overnight bag, went back into the bedroom and told her, "I'll be back for my things tomorrow, but I want you to understand—this is final. I can't force you to give me a divorce, but you can't force me to stay with you."

She said nothing. He made his way through the bedroom, past the library, the living room, the dining room, subconsciously saying good-bye to the surroundings that had been home, even if shared with someone incompatible. He paused for a moment in the small room next to the housekeeper's, which he had fixed up for himself as a study, the walls lined with medical books and files. Tomorrow he would get in touch with Mrs. Tummler's nephew, who had done the carpentering for him. The boy had a small truck; he could pack and move the things to his office in the hospital. He thought of knocking on the housekeeper's door to tell her to give Heinrich the message, then realized it was almost three o'clock. Too late to disturb the old lady.

He took the elevator down to the garage, got his car, stepped on the gas and drove up the ramp, turning sharply to the right as he emerged, and almost ran over Helene.

She was crouched in his path, in her nightgown, a coat thrown over her shoulders. The brakes screeched as he brought the car to a violent stop that almost catapulted him into the windshield. He couldn't see beyond the hood, but he had felt no impact and knew he hadn't touched her.

He jumped out of the car, torn by a rage he had never experienced before. "You damn fool! What are you trying to do? There are easier ways of committing suicide, without involving your husband. Or was that what you wanted?"

The crouched figure didn't move. Windows in the building above opened, lights went on, people appeared on balconies, peering down into the street, roused by the screeching of the brakes and his loud, furious voice.

"Get out of my way."

But Helene didn't move.

"Get up!" He wanted to kick her but controlled himself. She began to scream, long, agonized screams, her face upturned. He slapped her, hard, as he would have slapped an hysterical patient—once, twice. She lurched forward face down on the ground.

Suddenly a neighbor from their floor was at his side. "You shouldn't have hit her. Even if she did whore around. But she's a woman."

He couldn't recall ever having seen the man before. He lunged at the man, knocking him down. All at once there was a police car, the blue lights on its roof spinning in the gray dawn, and two policemen in black uniforms and white helmets, and questions he couldn't answer.

"Hysterical," was all he could say. "She was hysterical."

"And with good reason," a woman's voice cut in, a woman like Helene, in a nightgown, a coat covering her shoulders. And to one of the officers, "She's crazy about him while he's running around with . . ." and somebody interrupting her, "I guess a man can get away with anything if he's famous," and a police officer's calm voice, "Seeing that nothing has happened that is any concern of ours, I think you'd better take the Frau Professor back up to where she belongs," and a hand on his shoulder, "We all have our problems."

The men half carried her to the elevator, along the corridor, to her bed, her feet dragging as if paralyzed. "She's fainted."

"No, she hasn't," Zeller snapped at the officer who was lowering her onto the bed with fatherly concern. "Damn her! We have only one life, and to throw it away . . ."

He didn't notice their leaving. He counted her pulse, he took her blood pressure. All normal. Her eyelids fluttered. There was nothing wrong with her. "Don't you dare try this sort of thing again," he said in a low voice.

"If you leave me," she said, "I shall try it again. I shall find a way . . ."

He turned his back on her, went into the library and called the senior resident of the cardiology department. "Dr. Adermann? I intended to come back but I couldn't make it. Will you please look in on 505. If there's anything unexpected, the slightest abnormality . . ."

How could he have forgotten to look in on the man? It was Lisa's fault. Lisa's. Helene's. And both of them had said the same thing—that he was an egoist who made neither of them happy. Both threatening him with a different sort of separation, typical for each of them: Lisa's dignified, Helene's psychotic.

He threw himself on the bed in the guest room, too distracted to undress. To live without Lisa was out of the question; to continue to live with Helene was equally impossible. To have her own husband kill her. To threaten suicide as an answer to losing a man she didn't love. And there was no consoling doubt in his mind that she meant it, however crazily dramatic her next attempt might be. He was caught between a wife he had to be rid of and a girl he needed. And he understood neither.

He turned out the light. In the dark, thinking could become unbearable. Lisa would have no understanding for Helene's kind of blackmail. Indecent, she'd call it. She wouldn't believe Helene meant it. But she did. Perhaps he had known it all along, perhaps that was why he hadn't insisted on a divorce before. Or was he just finding excuses for himself? For not being able to come to a decision. He, who had to make vital decisions every day, decisions over life and death. To operate or not to operate. How deep to cut. What to remove. Taking risks not only for himself but for others. But as a man with women?

Indecisive. Or just arrogant enough to believe that with all the important work he did, he could afford to be lax as a human being?

He thought of calling Lisa to tell her that he had never been unfaithful to her. But was that true? It was, unless you wanted to count that time during a lecture tour. Every night in a different city, every night in another hotel, and the little Irish girl had said, "Your ties are all crumpled; want me to iron them?" In an irresistible brogue. "Black hair, blue eyes, long black lashes, and very full breasts," he had told Lisa, which had made it seem less unfaithful, and she had laughed, "As long as I'm not around . . ." But would she understand that he would always feel like a murderer if Helene killed herself?

How could a woman want a man who didn't love her? Never had. He wanted to go into the bedroom and tell her that he had never loved her, but felt too exhausted to move. Bitch, he thought. Lisa, too, was a bitch. Seeing Chris Chase on the side. And what about proud, cool

Helene whoring around? Suddenly, the man's words outside registered. Well, good for her. If it was true, *he* could divorce *her*. But of course the very idea was absurd.

He got up, went into the living room, put on a record. Bach. But Bach wouldn't do. Orff was what he needed. But he couldn't find the Orff where the heads of young nuns fell under the axe. He found some early Beatles and turned on the volume so loud, it threw the music and the words back from the wall. The phone rang. Complaint. Well, naturally. He turned the volume down and fell asleep on the couch.

5

Christopher Chase liked being posted in Zurich. The cleanliness of the city appealed to him, as did its international atmosphere of high finance that attracted so many interesting and illustrious people. He enjoyed walking down the Bahnhofstrasse—the richest street in the world, according to the guides—especially in July, when the overpowering scent of linden blossoms went to your head. And the lakes so close; and the mountains nearby for skiing. Paris, Munich, London, only a hop away. You could get almost anywhere in no time if you wanted a change of atmosphere, people, food, climate. And like Lisa he loved the church bells ringing in Sundays—Sankt Peter, Grossmünster, Fraumümster. They gave him a sense of peace, as did the city itself with its orderly, unrushed way of life. Others might find it boring, but it suited him.

"So what's your choice?" he asked, steering Lisa to the right where he had parked his car, and at the same time trying to curb his dog. They were coming out of an early movie, an American musical which she hadn't found very amusing. Still, it was better than sitting at home alone. Dogs were allowed in Zurich's movie houses, except on weekends. You parked them in the checkroom, something Chris appreciated highly.

"The Storchen, the Baur au Lac, or the Kronenhalle?"

His German was excellent; he had mastered even the complications of the Zurich dialect.

"I don't want you to spend so much money on me," said Lisa.

"That's my business. You like the Kronenhalle best, don't you?"

It was one of the most impressive restaurants in the world. Others might be grander, more luxurious, with a more breathtaking view, but the walls of the Kronenhalle were covered with masterpieces—Picasso, Braque, Degas, Monet, Rouault, Chagall—and to sit there, gazing at them and at the same time eat and be served with concern and speed, had always been a treat.

He opened the door of his car, but she shook her head. "I'd like to walk. You mind?"

They left the dog in the car. "Let's cross on the Münster Bridge," she said.

It was her favorite crossing of the Limmat, the river that issued from Lake Zurich and divided the city. Here the view on both banks and in both directions was perhaps the most traditional and the least disturbed by shops, although she would never reconcile herself to the "Omega" and "Tissot" signs, brightly illuminated against a low wall behind which rose the imposing twin-towered Romanesque cathedral. The incongruity of modern stores, modern traffic, and modern dress against the many buildings built for a quite different era . . . useless to see it that way. The two couldn't be made to match. As they passed the Fraumünster, Chris saluted Bürgermeister Hans Waldman, the fifteenth-century warrior-mayor of Zurich, astride his bronze horse with its beautiful green patina, and Lisa had to smile. His appreciation of the romanticism of her city was one of the most appealing things about him. The Galerie Spink monopolized the Hechtplatz, but with its neat cobblestones and stone fountain in the center, the little square was less marred than most of the many old-world spots. The gray stone youth atop his pedestal, tugging at his huge pike, his feet lost in a cushion of geraniums, petunias, and overflowing vines, looked down at the many cars parked all around him. He had been there long before them and seemed to say that he would be there long after they were gone. In a country that had never been ruined by war, all monuments seemed destined to live forever.

At the corner of busy Rämistrasse, the Kronenhalle faced them, its old lamps subduedly lit. To her surprise, she found that he had reserved a table. "How did you know I'd want to come here?"

"I didn't. I simply made reservations in all your favorites. So excuse me for a moment while I cancel the others."

Their table was against a window. Chris preferred to sit against a wall rather than out in the open where waiters could bump into you and the conversation was encompassing and noisy. "No drink for me," she told him. "I have to be on duty at six tomorrow."

Sudden dejection showed in his face, "Why do you choose to go out with me only when you're under a time limit?"

"I'm often tired after a long day's work. You should remember that."

"I also remember that after a two-hour nap you are ready for anything." He repeated, "Anything."

He held out the menu, but she couldn't concentrate on it. His words had stung her. He was the first man she'd gone to bed with steadily.

"Order for me, please."

He did. Then he asked, "Still assisting Zeller?"

"Of course. I've never let personal relationships interfere with my work. You wouldn't either."

"Oh, I don't know," he said dispiritedly, which at once made her feel sorry for him. He was toying with his hair, which he wore brushed back to a few inches below the ears. It was naturally wavy, and with his sharply chiseled features it gave him a rather angelic look. The saving grace, in her opinion, was that it was prematurely sprinkled with gray. She thought this gave him character, but it bothered him; he thought it made him look old. He wasn't quite thirty, yet sometimes he seemed to think of himself as an old man.

How typically American it was, this obsession with youth, with the uselessness of old age. And how much they missed by rejecting their elders, with all their acquired wisdom. In that respect they could learn from the Chinese with whom there was suddenly such amity. But they wouldn't. They had this inflated idea that only they could be the teachers. Of what? All thoughts she couldn't discuss with Chris.

A very hot soup came. She looked down at it rather as if she didn't know what to do with it. "Go on. Eat it. You look undernourished."

She took a few spoonfuls while he drank his martini. "No wine, please," she told him, as he was about to order a bottle.

"Then I'll have a second martini." And when the drink came, "Lisa, did you tell him?"

"Yes."

"And his reaction?"

"He thought I'd gone crazy and stormed out."

"So that's the end?"

She hunched her shoulders, let them drop, stopped eating. "I don't know."

His mind was so one-track. She wondered if she would always be involved with men who didn't understand women. "I've made up my mind not to see him again, privately, that is, but that doesn't mean I'll marry you tomorrow."

"I'm to be put on ice because maybe he'll be back?"

"If that's the way you want to put it."

"At least you're honest."

"Shouldn't I be?"

"By all means. You know, when you told me it was all over between us, I was absolutely miserable. Then there were other girls, here and there, now and then, but none of them was as honest as you."

A veal cutlet arrived. She looked down at it with disgust. "Well, eat the mushrooms," he said, cutting into his steak.

"He called me today," she told him. "He said he'd come to an agreement with his wife. She wants him to stay with her three more months. Then, if he still wants a divorce, she'll let him have it."

"And you believe that?"

She shrugged. "What are three months after waiting three years?"

He put down his knife and fork. "In other words, you're going to wait out these three months."

She took a swallow of the water he always ordered

with a meal. Usually she didn't touch it, now she drank the whole glass. "I'm afraid so."

"I wish you cared that much for me."

"I care for you. But our relationship is different. Chris, you don't have to wait for me, in fact I don't want you to. I'll understand if you decide never to see me again. You don't even have to call me."

All through the time with Zeller, Chris had called her every month, always on the first. She had never known such pedantic devotion. Perhaps it was the lawyer in him, who couldn't let a client slip away. She stared at the large, almost totally blue Chagall. What made Chris so agreeable also made him in certain ways a bore. About him there was none of the exhilaration that emanated from Zeller, who could talk about the most ordinary things and make them sound fascinating. Zeller was the charged electric wire, Chris the sturdy wooden pole against which one could lean. The born friend every woman should have. Why couldn't she be satisfied with what he had to give?

"Chris, forget me, please. I've no right to keep you hanging around."

"You never did. You came right out with it. And believe me, there were quite a few times when I wished I'd never met you. At least eat your salad."

She poked around in the artichoke hearts and asparagus. "I'm sorry if you thought sending him away meant marrying you."

His face was calm again. It usually was. A lawyer's face, Toni had said once, shaped by law school. Manners and expression too. "You realize . . . I mean, a man's patience has its limits."

"I won't blame you."

"You're a courageous girl, sending two men packing within one week."

"I'm not sending you packing. I never would. You're my friend, my good friend. It's only that I have no right to hold out any hope, no matter what happens at the end of three months."

"My bad luck that you don't love me."

"It's just that I love him more."

"Why?"

"Oh Chris . . . what a hopeless question. How do I know why?"

The dessert came. She forced down a few spoonfuls, then looked at her watch. "Time for me to go."

He walked her to her house. Neither of them spoke. He didn't ask to come up.

6

At five in the morning, the alarm rang. Zeller jumped out of bed, stormed into the bathroom and turned on the shower full force. Ice cold. In the kitchen he heated the coffee Mrs. Tummler had made the night before. He clattered with cup and saucer, he banged doors shut, not because he wanted to disturb Helene but simply because he didn't give a damn.

He stopped in the Winterthurerstrasse. The front door opened and Lisa slipped silently into the seat beside him. They had hardly spoken to each other since the night she had sent him away, and several times Sister Regina had taken her place in the operating room.

"Filthy temper," she had reported. "What in the world has happened between the two of you?"

Regina was her closest friend, still Lisa had offered no information.

But last night he had called her. "I have to go out to Maur tomorrow. Coming? Or would you rather have me ask Regina?"

She knew how he would hate to have a third person see what he was doing. "Of course I'll come," she told him. It would be childish to let their personal difficulties interfere with his work. Besides, she ached to see him.

They didn't speak on the way. Was his mind so intensely concentrated on what lay ahead, or was he still angry with her? They turned in at the gate; he parked his car in front of the cow barn and went on ahead. She followed him, almost at a trot, to the ell he had built on for the slaughtering of the calves. As they reached the door, the butcher came out. *"Gruetzi,"* he said. "Everything's ready for you."

"Thank you, Hannes," said Zeller. "I can always rely on you."

In the left corner of the room was a large sink. From the cupboard underneath it Zeller took a bottle of pHisohex and several brushes wrapped in plastic, while Lisa gave her hands an antiseptic scrub. He watched her—just for a moment, but she felt it. He opened a plastic drum and took out two white gowns, freshly laundered and still smelling of detergent; he took a stainless-steel box down from a shelf. It contained several surgical knives which he avoided touching. Lisa walked over to the drum, dried her hands on the sterile towel, slipped into one of the gowns, and Zeller tied the strings at the back for her. While she struggled into surgical gloves, he put on his cap and gown. His gloves were at the bottom of the drum. It was all routine, a silent ballet.

The calf was still warm. Lisa handed Zeller the forceps with the gauze sponge clipped into it. He extended one hand and she poured a red, antiseptic solution over the sponge. After two minutes of scrubbing the calf's skin, he removed the sponge; Lisa replaced it with a fresh one. The same procedure was repeated, after which Zeller opened the calf with a large scalpel, beginning at the distal end of the abdomen, through the breastbone and into the chest. Lisa had taken up her position beside him and now held the chest of the animal open with two surgical hooks. With large scissors Zeller removed the thymus gland and placed it in a glass container filled with a light liquid. With a pair of forceps he then severed one of the large arteries running from the heart and loosened it from the surrounding tissue as far down as the kidneys. By a transverse cut he obtained an approximately six-inch piece of the animal's aorta. It too was placed in a glass container, after which both containers were closed with a tight-fitting lid. Zeller began to hum. In the hospital he was known to hum during an operation, a sign that things were going well.

Zeller looked at his watch. "One hour and twenty minutes. Not bad."

They crossed over to the house and went straight to the lab in the basement. It was sparsely equipped. There was none of the distracting clutter of rubber hoses, Bunsen burners, flasks, retorts, test tubes, and wooden stands, none of the mysterious looking glass cylinders or jars of chemicals and multicolored powders. While Zeller slipped into a fresh sterile gown, donned a mask and cap, and put on sterile gloves, Lisa spread a sterile towel on one of the two laboratory tables and laid out on it the basic surgical instruments: forceps, scissors, several scalpels. She opened the two glass containers that held the specimen of the calf. Four sterilized blenders were standing on the other table. She filled two with sterile water, the other two with peanut oil. Zeller cut the aorta into several pieces and divided them equally, then tossed one pile into the water, the other into the oil. He went through the same procedure with the thymus gland. Then he closed the four blenders and switched them on.

His original hope had been that if either of the biological specimens contained an active substance to combat atherosclerosis, it could be water or oil soluble. In any case, the actual obtaining of a solution ready for injecting was comparatively simple; dosage and effect were the mysteries.

From the start, a little more than two years ago, he had experimented mainly on monkeys because anatomically they came closest to human beings. They didn't suffer from atherosclerosis; they had to be fed fat to induce it, after which one could work to reduce the fatty deposits in their arteries. Soon they were exhibiting the unmistakable signs of AS, not only in autopsy material but also in their sluggish behavior and in classical changes in their electrocardiograms. He started his series of injections, only to discover that the high content of foreign protein in the first emulsions made it impossible to keep the animals alive over the period of time necessary to prove the efficacy, if any, of the injected preparation. The unavoidable immune reaction against the foreign protein was killing his animals as fast as he treated them. In order to eliminate the foreign protein factor as much as possible, and hoping that the effective elements would remain in the solution, he had had the idea of putting his "blender product" through a sterile centrifuge to separate the heavy particles from the lighter solution on top. And it did so. He then filtered the solution through a regular filter paper in several layers. In this way he was able to create a fairly clear suspension from both the aqueous and oily preparations. And he was ready to start again. This time, combining the solutions with small doses of cortisone, he was able to keep most of his animals alive, although he observed in many of them high temperature and chills, lasting about twenty-four hours.

He had divided the animals into three groups of ten. All of them were the same age and had been on the same diet and showed by and large the same degree of AS and almost identical EKG patterns. He sacrificed one animal in each group and obtained a careful autopsy report from the pathology department of the hospital, this to assure himself that he actually was working on animals with far-advanced pathology.

The material was injected into the three groups. Group one received both the aqueous and oil extracts of the aorta; group two the oil and aqueous extracts of the thymus; group three, the aqueous and oil extracts of aorta and thymus. Injections were given every three days.

In groups one and two the mortality rate remained unchanged. Two of the animals died of cardiovascular disease, the rest remained sluggish, and the EKGs, which were taken regularly, showed signs of further deterioration. From group three, however, he didn't lose a single animal. On the contrary, their EKGs showed considerable improvement. The animals appeared alert and friendlier, their cholesterol level had fallen from 300–350mg% to the more acceptable level of 220mg%. Their lipoproteins were within normal limits.

It was almost certain that the combination of aorta and thymus from young animals did indeed contain an effective x factor that not only prevented the formation of atherosclerosis plugs, but also had the capacity to dissolve plugs that were already present in the diseased vascular system. A complete recanalization of the system could be achieved. He was on the brink of a great discovery.

The next step had been to find a human guinea pig, and a little over a year ago one had turned up, a strange-looking man who had consulted him as a patient. According to the man's medical history, AS was progressing at a frightening rate, the cholesterol level was incredibly high. After some hesitation, Zeller told him about an untried vaccine, and the man, knowing he was doomed, had given his permission to try it out on him, in spite of the admitted risk involved. Zeller and the man had been lucky. The man, called Schmidt, had not only survived, but over a period of six months his fatty plaques had begun to dissolve. Zeller would have liked to keep track of him, but Schmidt had disappeared at the conclusion of the treatments, only to turn up again a couple of months ago, fit as could be, much to Zeller's delight, with the request that Zeller treat a friend of his with the vaccine that had done him so much good. Zeller had turned him down when he had heard that the anonymous friend was in some way important. At that point he was still hesitant about trying it out on prisoner volunteers, however eager. The man had been quite persistent and had come back once more, only to be refused again.

The next person on whom Zeller had tried his vaccine was a volunteer from a prison in Basel. He had died after the first injection. So had the third, also a convict volunteer, even though Zeller had changed the formula. This was a few days before Schmidt's last visit. The fourth, the prisoner from Regensdorf on whom he had operated a few weeks ago after having treated him for several months with again a new combination, was still alive, his sclerotic condition improved.

This had brought him up to par, which didn't satisfy him. In his opinion—and here no other opinion counted —the vaccine was not yet ready to be turned over to an organic chemist for analysis and production. As he had told Lisa on that miserable evening—Enrico would have to wait.

For approximately fifteen minutes the blades of the blenders did their work. Zeller looked at his watch, switched them off, and could see in both a milky emulsion. He poured it into the glass containers, sealed them and put them in the freezer. With its temperature set at the lowest level, organic contents were good for three days.

He turned his key in the new lock he had had put on the freezer, also on the door to the lab. "Thank you for coming," he said to Lisa as they left together. He thought he could see tears in her eyes, but all she said was, "I was glad to." Neither of them noticed a small Italian sports car start off after the Cadillac; the only one who did was a man, smoking a French cigarette, behind the wheel of a small red Peugeot.

7

Helene had taken up golf seriously. To her susprise she had developed into an expert player. There was strength in her arms, and her broad hips rotated as easily as a loose wheel. She never lifted her head, even during her first lesson she had kept her eyes on the ball through her swing, never changing her stance and concentrating on the green as if her life depended on sending the ball into the cup with one stroke. Her teacher was proud of her and had promised that in three years she would be winning club tournaments in Switzerland. She played ambitiously. She knew very well that she was striving to outdo Anton in some kind of field.

Whenever possible she played early in the morning at the Dolder Grand. She rammed a tee into the ground and placed her ball. Zeller had scarcely spoken a word to her since the night she had thrown herself in front of his car. Her promise to give him a divorce after three months, if he still wanted it then—a promise she had no intention of keeping—hadn't changed anything. "Blackmail!" he had spat out at her last night when she had tried to be civil and start some sort of conversation.

From her point of view it wasn't blackmail. Her uncontrolled emotions should have revealed to him how desperately she needed him, always had, ever since she had won him. That was how she had seen it then and how she saw it now—he was her trophy. She had taken him home to

Houston like a prize. You didn't let a trophy go, especially when it was the only one you had.

He, of course, saw everything through a man's mentality. Men! She had never been interested in men. In sex, yes. But sex wasn't love. The confusion of sex and love . . . if she had a paper to write today, that would be her theme. And because this was the way she saw it, she hadn't cared about his escapades. He had to relieve himself, so what? And she? The man who had upbraided Zeller for slapping her, "even if she whores around," hadn't been wrong. The butcher boy was pretty, and some of the other young men who delivered to their apartment were equally desirable and satisfactory. How like Anton to knock the man down. This was something his male ego couldn't accept as true. The place where he had slapped her, slapped her like a child in a tantrum, still burnt. *Coram publico.* She was going to make him pay for that. She sent the ball flying, a good two hundred yards.

At the sixth hole a young man was teeing off. Handsome. Looked English. Hair an inch long in the back, a mustache, very *soigné*, giving his narrow lips a certain importance.

He stepped back politely. "If you want to pass . . ."

"Thanks, I can wait." And a moment later, "Seeing you playing by yourself . . . why not play together?"

"But you're so much better than I am. I was watching you. I'm only a beginner. I'd hold you up."

"Never mind."

He stepped aside and let her tee up. For the first time in ages, she sliced. His ball went straight, but only a short distance. Still, she had a par while he was three strokes over.

"English?" she asked, on the seventh tee.

"British."

Naturalized, she decided, born in India, or in one of the colonies Great Britain had relinquished so gracefully after the war.

"And you?"

"Swiss."

"Wouldn't have thought so."

"What did you think I was?"

He gave her a very intense look, head slightly to one side. "You could be Italian. Or Spanish."

50

For no good reason she could think of, it flattered her to be taken for a Latin. Perhaps because it would have annoyed her parents. She also enjoyed his surprise when she told him, "Actually I'm Swiss only by marriage. I'm American. From Texas."

"Well, I'd never have guessed that," said the young man. "You don't have an accent."

She smiled. The fellow made her feel almost carefree. She hadn't thought she still had it in her.

"I was a student here. Psychology," she told him, then regretted having mentioned her major. She didn't want to scare him off. "And I stayed."

Drops of perspiration were forming on her forehead. She usually perspired when sexually excited. Anton had hated it. She wiped her forehead.

"What about a second round?" he asked, as they ended up near the hotel.

"Perhaps later. What I'd like now is a drink."

"May I invite you?"

They sat on the oval terrace in front of the Dolder dining room. Both ordered Bloody Marys. "I'm sorry. I didn't introduce myself before. Graham Foley."

"And I'm Mrs. Zeller. Mrs. Anton Zeller."

"The heart surgeon?"

She nodded, gratified. There was rarely anyone who didn't recognize her husband's name.

"Then you're a famous woman."

"I'm the wife of a famous man, let's put it that way."

"You must be enormously proud."

"I am."

He sent his drink back because it wasn't sufficiently spiced. "Of course I guess fame has its price. I've been told he's been hounded ever since he began his research on atherosclerosis. He's had some success with the results, hasn't he? If he finds a way to arrest it, it would be a miracle."

Everybody was always talking about Anton as if she didn't exist, even this young man on whom she thought she had made an impression.

"He believes in miracles, and that may do it." She smiled. "And what do you do?"

"I paint."

"Successfully?"

"If you mean, do I enjoy it? Yes. If you mean can I make it pay? No."

It made her laugh. "I'm going for a swim. I always bring my suit along. How about you?"

"Good idea. I'll buy some trunks."

They walked to the swimming pool, one of nearly Olympic length. At certain intervals it made waves. Illusions of the ocean. They changed and swam for about twenty minutes. When she came out of her cabin in a dry suit, he was waiting for her, sitting at one of the tables, shaded by a gay umbrella. White terrycloth shorts, a towel slung over his shoulder. Again she had to admire how marvelously he was built. He got up and took her hand and held it loosely. In a strange way it made her feel one with him. Together they walked down the broad stone steps where people were sunning, across the grass, past several refreshment stands. At the last booth he bought a bottle of soda water. "Swimming always makes me thirsty," he said.

They crossed a meadow where children were playing and grown-ups lay on towels or sat in chairs. Facing them was dark, dense woods. "Where are we going?" she asked. He didn't answer, he just looked at her for a moment, then led her to where a narrow footpath cut in among the trees.

The path was shady and cool. After a short while he led her off it and they walked deeper into the woods. Suddenly there was a clearing. He spread out his towel for her and they sat down. He opened the bottle, offered it to her, she shook her head and he drank almost half of it. She watched the movement of his throat and began to tremble.

He took her then and there, and he was good. Or was she just so feverishly ready? He was rough—the way he grasped her thighs and parted her legs, his strong thrust. Anton had never been rough. And it was the first time she had made love in the open. The smell of the firs, the earth, themselves. A light breeze passing between their sweating bodies. The play of leafy shadows on their naked skins. The drunken tumble of a butterfly on his body, crushing hers into the ground.

52

They took a second dip which she hoped to God would calm her. But it didn't. "Don't call me," she told him. But he did. The next day.

Eight days of bliss, of a satisfaction she had never experienced before. He had only to touch her hand and she came close to a climax, and when he took his knowing fingers away, it left her trembling with a desire that was invariably fulfilled. Over and over again.

But there was more. The story of his miserable youth, of his frustration trying to hold on to the one thing that gave meaning to his life, moved her deeply. She could picture him, selling his paintings on Paris street corners to pay for his art studies, paintings for which he could hardly afford oil and canvas. And then thrown out suddenly into nowhere, trying his hand at jobs he was no good at. There was also an almost childlike heedlessness about him, the way he plunged into things without thought of possible consequence. It made her feel protective, almost responsible. She had known boys who made her feel this way, but never a man.

On the eighth day, picnicking on a meadow, he mentioned Zeller again. "Don't," she said. "Don't spoil our time. I'm so happy to forget him. You make me forget him."

"Why do you want to forget him?"

Oh God, the reasons she could have given and finally, to her surprise, did—the hurts she had suffered and some that she hadn't even admitted to herself. When she had finished she realized that he was the first person to whom she had revealed herself.

He took her face in both hands and lifted it to his. His sudden tenderness moved her, and she burst into tears. He caressed her gently. "Cry," he said, "it will do you good." After a while he took his handkerchief and wiped her tears away and drew her close, as if she were a child.

"I'm sorry," she said.

"Don't be sorry. I'm more grateful than I can say for your confidence. There's just one thing you haven't made clear to me. If you are so unhappy, why won't you give him a divorce?"

"Why do you think?"

He smiled. "Because you can't bear the thought of his finding happiness with somebody else."

"Perhaps."

"But you may have to."

"What do you mean?"

"We've been seen."

"We've been seen? By whom?"

"The man at the booth where I bought the soda water, the day we met. He recognized you, and he followed us. He's made his demands pretty clear. Your husband could get a divorce on that."

An icy fear knifed down her spine. This was a danger she had never taken into consideration. How stupid you could be when you wanted something badly. But she had always been cautious . . . until now. She had made certain that her housekeeper was out when she was expecting one of the boys, and fortunately she had avoided anyone in their own set, where scandals were always difficult to avert, and any of Anton's colleagues. What if Anton took her to court? But would he be willing to expose their private affairs in public? There was even less chance, though, of his giving in to blackmail. There it was again . . . blackmail.

Graham Foley said, "You look appalled."

"I am. I don't think I could face being a middle-aged divorcée."

He said, "You don't have to be. I'm in love with you, Helene. I want to marry you."

She was shocked, yet at the same time deliriously gratified. The totally surprising thought of sharing her life with him opened up a future she had never dreamed possible. A future with a man not tied to a time-consuming, all-absorbing profession, a man for whom sex was not only an act of relief and relaxation, but an art. And it occurred to her that this man would be more or less financially dependent on her, and that was a stimulating prospect. She could help him in his career, and unlike Zeller he would appreciate it. She knew people who could afford to buy his work or have their portrait painted; she could arrange exhibitions for him. Already she saw herself as his patron.

"You look happier."

"I'd like to see your work," she said.

He laughed. "Does your answer depend on how good I am?"

"No. But suddenly I want to know all about you."

"All right. Tomorrow I'll take you to my studio. Meanwhile, think about it. Promise?"

She said nothing. She didn't have to. She looked at him and his hands were where she longed to feel them. "Hurt me," she whispered.

The next three days passed without a call from him. She was almost out of her mind, but managed not to show it. In her desperation she called him at the Savoy every hour, even at night when Anton was asleep. He was always out. Had anything happened to him? She thought of trying the hospital, the police. Then, unexpectedly, his voice on the phone. No apology, no excuse, just, "I've got to see you."

At first she almost said no, then the relief of hearing his voice, of knowing that he was alive, swept away all anger over the anxiety he had caused her.

They met at the zoo. It was a weekday morning and there were few visitors. He was waiting for her at the entrance, leaning cross-legged against the stone drinking fountain topped by a crouched lion. He had already bought the tickets, and as she passed him he handed her one. She walked through the gate and he followed her to the flamingo pit, where they stood and watched the ungainly birds stalking on their long thin legs that looked so brittle. They started to walk along the main path. "Let's go in," he said, as they passed the Reptile House.

She shook her head. "I hate snakes. I have a phobia about them. I can't stand anything that creeps silently. I'd rather be eaten by a tiger than bitten by a snake."

"Then let's sit down."

"No, I'd rather walk."

They turned left, up the long flight of stone steps that led past the monkeys, and paused for a moment to watch them leaping from boulder to boulder in their huge cage. One, sitting close to the bars, looked at her almost mockingly. He would never get himself into such a predicament, the wise little face seemed to say. That was for humans.

A right turn past the tigers, royal beasts. Her heart was beginning to beat normally again. Here, on the upper level, peacocks were perched on the red-tiled roof of a building, their ugly strident cries piercing the air. Crates of fresh lettuce stood on the ground, snow white peacock pigeons fluttering around them. In the distance the sound of rifle fire, someone target shooting, surprisingly loud in the clear air. For no good reason, the sound made her shudder.

"I thought you were going to show me your stduio," she said. "Why did we have to meet here?"

"There is no studio, Helene," he said, "and I have to go away."

She was too shocked to move on. "Go away? Why?" She grasped his arm. "You can't go away. You can't leave me."

"I don't want to leave you, but there's nothing I can do about it. Unless you help me."

"Help you? How? You know I'd do anything . . ."

He took her arm and propelled her on again slowly. "Helene—where does your husband keep the data on his findings?"

"The data on his findings?" Astonishment made her stammer. "What have Anton's findings got to do with us?"

"Everything."

"I don't understand. What in God's name are you talking about?"

He led her along a path that curved upward to a terrace patio with a stone parapet facing the parklike animal scene below, and on the opposite side, a stone bench, backed by leafy bushes. "Let's sit down," he said.

For a while he said nothing, then he told her, "It all started years ago. I'd hit rock bottom, I had debts, and there was a man who wanted me to do a job for him."

"Such as?"

"A dirty job. Spying. Stealing. It pays surprisingly well."

Her eyes widened. "Gram! How could you get mixed up in anything like that?"

"That's a question I've asked myself many times. Perhaps it's too much to expect you to understand what it means to have nothing, not only no money, but no *one*.

56

I tried to break away, but they always found me, and they had enough on me to put me behind bars if I refused. And now they want Zeller's secret."

Her mind went blank with the preposterousness of the situation. "But . . . you can't get it. He keeps everything in our safe in his study, and it's burglar-proof."

"That's why I said you must help me."

"Impossible!"

"You don't understand. It's a question of life and death. My life."

He was very pale. "Don't exaggerate," she said, trying to still her sudden fear.

"I am not exaggerating," he said, so calmly that she had to believe him. "I have three more days. If I don't deliver by then, they'll put another man on the job and that will be the end of me. My only chance is to leave as quickly as possible and hope they don't track me down."

He got up and began to pace the small secluded area. He was afraid. She could see that he was trembling. Graham gone. Graham dead. It was inconceivable.

She went over to where he was standing, his back turned. "I couldn't possibly do it," she said.

He swung around to face her. "Then I'll do it for you."

"How?"

"You'll give me the combination and I'll come to the apartment."

"But what if he's home? I never know when he's going to be home."

"I'll come tomorrow night. At two. Shortly before that there'll be a call from Maur. I'll see to it that something happens that takes him out there. No blame will fall on you. I'll make it look like a burglary. All you have to do is unlock the front door after he's gone. Put the combination in your pocketbook and leave it in the library. Your jewelry will be gone—don't worry, you'll get it back—and maybe the television set and the radio, and I'll break the lock as I leave to make it look plausible."

Suddenly she couldn't force back the suspicion. What if he was only after her jewelry? "You've thought of everything, haven't you?"

"Had to. I can't afford to risk anything now that I have you. Helene, I love you."

"But we'll have these . . . these horrible men on our necks all our lives."

"No," he said. "This is my last job. I've been promised that."

He pinned her against the parapet, his body moving against hers. Their lips met. She had never been kissed that way before, not even by him. So it had to end here, in a public park, with her starved for him?

"Three weeks from today," he said, "we meet at the Ritz, in Paris."

Helene sat down on the stone bench again. That he wasn't with her didn't register. She took a deep breath. "But what you are asking me to do is a crime," she said, in a voice barely above a whisper, her unseeing eyes looking straight ahead. "I can't do it, and I can't help you do it. That would be just as terrible as death. And it has nothing to do with Anton, who would see his life's work taken from him. I simply don't have it in me. I've been raised too conventionally. I couldn't live with myself if I did it. I know you're going to say I've done things that are just as bad, but they're not. Giving your body its natural fulfillment is not a crime . . ."

She looked around, expecting to find him sitting beside her. No one was there. "Gram," she called. "Where are you?" and felt the full impact of his absence. It was worse than death. It was worse than any crime. She couldn't face life without him, not now, when it had just begun. Oh God, where could she go to think?

She recalled that he had wanted to see the reptiles. It was feeding time and she forced herself to look for him around the glass cages. She left the zoo and drove to Sprüngli's, parked her car, walked into the sweetshop and up the stairs to the coffee shop on the second floor. The waitress pointed to a free table in a corner. Helene put her things down to indicate that it was taken, then went to the counter with its choice of beautiful little sandwiches and magnificent pastries. She chose a round slice of bread with salmon and a ring of egg on it, another on which asparagus tips were arranged, a strawberry tart. She went back to her table and told the waitress to bring her coffee with whipped cream. She knew she would be served the same sort of thing at five o'clock, at her daily bridge party, but she didn't care. A few women she knew were sitting at another table. She ignored them and buried her face in a newspaper she had bought at the cashier's desk. With her stomach filled, she felt calmer, although she couldn't concentrate on what she was reading. On her way out she stopped at the sweet counter downstairs and bought half a pound of marzipan and a pound of the sugar-coated almonds Anton loved. She looked at her watch, walked to where she had parked her car, but then crossed the street to the Savoy. He wasn't there. Wouldn't be back for two or three days. Did she care to leave a message?

On a small sheet of paper she wrote, "Impossible." Folded it. Tore it up.

"No message."

8

For two days Graham Foley had noticed a small red Peugeot following him. He didn't like it. Several times he had tried to throw it off, but just when he thought he had succeeded, there it was on his tail again. Whoever the driver was, he seemed to have an uncanny sense for Graham's destination. It made him so edgy that finally, finding himself on a seldom-traveled dirt road leading to one of the old peasant houses near Maur, he braked to a halt, blocking the Peugeot's way.

"Hello, Foley," said the man at the wheel. "I expected you to do this one of these days."

He was a slender, long-legged fellow, immaculately—one might have said foppishly—dressed, his tie a draped red bow sprinkled with white dots, as if a butterfly had settled on his throat. He took off his sunglasses. Aristocratic features, handsome, too handsome, almost pretty. Behind his amiable expression Graham could sense a sharper, cruel look. He had never seen the man before, and that the fellow knew his name startled him.

"Excuse me if I don't introduce myself at this point." The voice was soft, with a trace of warmth in it. He spoke perfect English, but with a definite French accent.

"All right. Why have you been tailing me?"

"I'm not tailing you; I'm sightseeing. The countryside is beautiful, don't you think so? Right here still so untouched by modern intrusions."

"Oh, come off it." Graham couldn't control the harshness in his voice. It maddened him because he knew it betrayed his fear. "Let's not play games."

"I was told to keep an eye on you."

Not by the police, thought Graham. They might well use people of other nationalities for detective work, but right now the police had nothing on him. In Switzerland his slate was clean. That was why he had been chosen for this job. By Smith? The talk he had had with Smith under the Monet rushed to his mind, lighting it up for a moment as if on a dark screen. Schmidt, Schmitt, Smith had been furious about his failure to produce, had threatened him. Had he engaged this man to take over his job? Was this the man who would eventually eliminate him?

The man didn't look like a killer, but then you could never tell. A gun with a silencer was simple to handle. He could follow Graham in his car, draw up alongside him, shoot him through the window—it had been done a thousand times.

"And who told you to keep an eye on me?"

"Somebody who doesn't like the man you're working for."

For a few seconds nothing was said. The two men stared at each other, Graham trying not to show his confusion, the other unblinking, his stare almost hypnotic. Then he slowly put on his glasses again.

When stalling for time, accuse. Graham had picked it up somewhere along this unhappy line of work. "Well, you're not very good at your job," he said. "A child would have noticed the way you were tailing me."

"I had my reasons," said the man, lighting a Gaulois. "But I needed the right opportunity to talk to you privately. If you hadn't forced me off the road just now, I would have made you stop."

"Talk about what?"

"Business."

"What about it?"

"Let's work together."

The careless way it was put convinced Foley. This man had not been hired by Smith. Nobody would have dared to propose a deal to double-cross Smith, not if he was in his service, unless it was to test Foley's loyalty. Still, he

61

took his time answering. Whatever the offer meant, haste could be disastrous.

"You mean against my employer?"

"How quickly you catch on. He treats you like dirt, doesn't he? And underpays you. He'll make a small fortune out of this, if you make it for him. I suggest you leave him out of it and we share the proceeds."

"Smith is a powerful man. I might never get around to enjoying—shall we call it the fruits of our labors? If he finds out I double-crossed him, I'm a dead man."

"I happen to know more powerful people than Smith. I can guarantee you protection. *If* we deliver."

The possibility of getting out from under Smith's control filled Graham with momentary elation.

"And just why do you need me?"

"You've been on this job longer than I have, and you seem to be getting warm. Am I right? You'll be satisfied with what I have to offer in return for your partnership. All we need now is a detailed plan, mine dovetailing with yours."

"And what if you . . ." he almost said "double-cross me," but swallowed the end of his sentence. The man was no fool.

"What if I double-cross you? Isn't that a risk both of us have to take? What tells me I can trust you? Nothing but my instinct. And that's something I've always relied on . . . to my advantage. You'll make twice as much with me."

Graham, hands in pocket, looked down at his feet. He found he could concentrate better with the man out of his line of vision. This offer, he told himself, had come when he was on the brink of success. There was little doubt in his mind but that he would have what Smith was after before the next dawn. There also seemed to be little doubt of this in the other's mind. Would partnership with this strange man make things simpler, or complicate them? No need to grope for the answer. The man knew everything. Graham had little choice but to take the risk and accept. However slight and foppish, the man evidently had a mind as keen as a blade and, if Graham refused, might turn out to be as formidable an enemy as Smith.

He looked up again and found the sight of his new partner almost reassuring. "It's a deal."

They shook hands. "Beaulieu," said the man. "Gustave Beaulieu."

They straightened out their cars and parked them neatly at the edge of a meadow, and began to talk.

9

Chris and Lisa had been walking along the lake in front of the Baur au Lac. The swans were slowly dying out because of the pollution, and Lisa regretted it fiercely. The proud birds had always reminded her of the fairy tales of her childhood, of the first ballet she had seen and loved, *Swan Lake*, and of the sad fate of royalty. Chris was walking her home. He didn't care for walking as much as she, who felt the need for exercise in the fresh air after her day's work; he would have preferred to take his car. Still they reached her apartment too soon for him. "May I come up for a nightcap?"

She hesitated. He had kept her company on many a lonely evening, but it wouldn't do any good to raise his hopes, which he finally seemed to have under control. She shook her head. "Another night. Regina is coming over to show me how to put in sleeves."

"Taking up sewing?"

"It's fun."

He had met Regina, a tall woman who didn't look her six feet because she moved so gracefully. She also looked rather mannish, and the dark hairs on her upper lip had given him the impression that she was passionate. It occurred to him suddenly that Lisa, not sleeping with Zeller or with him, might have found temporary consolation with her girl friend. God forbid, he thought, then smiled as he reflected, What a square I am. He brushed Lisa's cheek with his lips. The temptation to take her in his arms, to

64

feel her body against his, was so strong, he almost gave in to it, but the moment his arm grew tight around her shoulders, she broke away and was gone before he had a chance to try again. He turned on his heels and whistled for his dog, who was still inspecting the same spot on the curb.

Lisa walked up the first flight of stairs slowly. If she turned Chris down again and again, she would lose him. He had always had a typically American inferiority complex where women were concerned and wouldn't subject himself to her rejection forever. Nor did she want him to. But in spite of her frequent insistence that he find somebody else, she didn't want to lose him either. He was a comfort, perhaps because she too was not at all sure that Helene would stick to her bargain at the end of the three months.

On the second floor she put the key in the lock, turned it, and to her surprise found it unlocked. Regina had a key; she must have arrived before her.

"Regina?"

But there was no answer, and the entrance hall was dark. She always left one light burning when she went out, a habit from childhood when she had been afraid of the dark. So she stood in the entrance with the light from the corridor shining on her.

No violence, thought the man, hiding behind the kitchen door. Not if I can possibly help it. A pity. She looked soft and young, and he could have had a bit of fun with her. But orders were orders.

Lisa half turned. Maybe she could still catch Chris; maybe she should go down and wait for Regina in the street. But she decided against it. She was not going to behave like a coward. What could be wrong?

She switched on the light. Her room had been ransacked, closet doors and drawers open. And then she saw him—a small wiry man. He was holding a large envelope in one hand. Toni's notes and letters to her.

All she could feel was fury. "Drop that," she said.

The man didn't. Instead he tried to get past her through the still-open door, but Lisa blocked the way. She knew better than to struggle, yet something impelled her. "Give me back that envelope."

He sprang at her. The small wiry body was all muscle.

65

There was a knife in his hand. She turned to run, but the knife penetrated her back. Wounded, she still tried to fight. She tried to scream, but now there was a hand around her throat, making it impossible. And a second stab. Suddenly there was another man, fighting off her assailant. His seizing the envelope was the last thing she saw.

10

It was in the morning papers, and on the air. Muggings were still rare in Switzerland.

Helene read about the attack on Lisa Tanner. The name used to make her tremble with rage, now she felt nothing. Lisa Tanner was a memory as far back as childhood, the kind one put aside when one grew up. Nothing could have made her realize more strongly to what extent she had committed herself to Graham Foley.

Zeller came home shortly after eleven. She could hear the housekeeper ask, "Anything wrong, Herr Professor?" As if she didn't know. But the servant's pretense gave her courage. An example, rather. She wasn't going to be outdone by an employee. She went into the library because she knew he would come to his favorite room, a hideaway really, from which, by mutual understanding, she was usually banned when he was home.

He looked like a ghost. He didn't seem to see her. He went straight to the bar, an old Swiss cupboard, its doors carved in a linenfold pattern. When opened, the inside lit up, and the mirrors he had installed showed an array of different-sized glasses and bottles.

"There's no ice."

"Mrs. Tummler," she called. "Would you please bring some ice."

When the housekeeper came back with the ice, she had a letter in her hand. "This just came, special delivery," she said, "from Signor Martelli."

Zeller, too distracted to even thank her, threw the letter unopened onto his desk. At this point he couldn't cope with anything Enrico might have on his mind, however urgent. He poured himself a stiff drink. Helene said softly, "I'm sorry, Anton," and it came close to the truth. He didn't respond, and she went on in the same soft voice, "No matter how much I suffered from your relationship with her, I feel sorry for the girl."

Zeller said nothing. He was staring out the window, watching a car ferry ply from Horgen on the opposite side, through the haze that veiled the lake. Lisa had been brought in in a state of shock, her pulse weak, her blood pressure fifty over zero. Their first efforts, even before examination, had been to do everything possible to prevent respiratory failure. The examination showed the lung badly punctured, but that had not been the only problem. A laparotomy had revealed that a second stab had penetrated the spleen. It couldn't be sutured; the spleen would have to come out. Blood transfusions and intravenous fluids hadn't hastened her return to consciousness, although they had been able to bring her blood pressure up to a safer level. And Buerkli had insisted on waiting for her to come to for what had seemed to Zeller an eternity. Then he and another surgeon had operated. For three hours. They had pumped the air and blood from the pleural cavity, then put her on another machine to make the lung expand. . . . "I thought we'd never get going," Zeller said, not so much to Helene as to himself.

He had always warned people not to be present when someone dear to them was being operated on. Too often he had seen the adverse aftereffects on the patient as well as on the observer; an experience of intimacy that could embarrass the former and leave the latter with a traumatic memory. But when Buerkli had suggested that he wait outside, he had not been able to take his advice. Knowing it to be wrong, or certainly unnecessary, he had watched. Later, when she had been brought to recovery, he had sat beside her bed, making the nurses nervous, then finally followed her to her room, holding her limp hand. It would be a long time—if she pulled through—before her strength would be back to normal.

He paced the room, up and down, up and down. Helene

thought he would never stop. But he did, to pick up the phone. "Buerkli? Any change?" and repeated his colleague's words, "No change."

Helene saw the tears form in his eyes. They didn't streak down his cheeks; they just rested under his lids. He brushed them away, but they formed again.

It was dreadful to see a man cry. It was even more dreadful to see a man cry for another woman. All sympathy was erased and hatred filled her once more. She felt more at home with it. Still, seeing him fill his glass for the fourth time, she said, "Don't drink so much. It won't help."

Sometime during the afternoon, he left. Mrs. Tummler, returning from some late shopping, told her, "He went to the Fluntern church."

Anton, the atheist, going to church? Unbelievable.

"How do you know?"

"I was there. I went to pray for the poor girl."

She couldn't explain to herself why this infuriated her. Suddenly the whole world was against her. "You're fired."

"As of when?"

"As of this minute."

Mrs. Tummler disappeared. So much for servant loyalty. They never stood by you. She hadn't realized how fond Mrs. Tummler had been of Anton, that she would side with him. And her sympathy for "the poor girl," from a straitlaced Swiss! The poor adultress!

An hour later the woman came back, dressed to go out, carrying a small piece of luggage. "I've packed all my things. Heinrich will pick them up tomorrow. There's some cold lamb in the icebox, a cucumber salad, cheese, and what's left of the chocolate cake. In case Herr Professor wants to eat anything. You owe me ninety francs, but you can send me a check if it isn't convenient to pay me now."

Helene sat in the library alone and didn't know what to do. She poured herself some scotch and forced herself to drink it. She didn't care for hard liquor, but it was certainly more effective than wine. She went into the kitchen. Spotlessly clean. She opened the linen closet. Just as neat as she wanted it. Not an edge or a corner of a sheet or towel out of line. The silver gleamed in the drawer. She ran her finger over the back of a chair. It came away clean. Nobody could say she wasn't a good housewife. She wouldn't keep on anyone who wasn't scrupulously tidy. She supposed she'd have to find and train somebody else to look after Anton. She had three weeks . . .

She turned on the radio, but there was nothing new. She must have fallen asleep, because when she woke up it was dark. The radio was still going and Anton hadn't come home. Nine o'clock, plus a few minutes. Maybe he'd stay at the hospital all night again? She wished he would. It would make everything easier. Still, she'd better find out. It wouldn't do for him to come home just when . . . she shivered. She wasn't cut out for what lay ahead.

She went back to the kitchen, opened the icebox, took out the cold lamb, the salad, the cake. To eat might restore her vigor. She found she could eat. She went back to the library and sat in his chair, waiting. When should she call the hospital to find out if he was staying or coming home? Eleven? Twelve? Time was a strange thing. Sometimes it rushed past you, you couldn't keep up with it, then it would stand still. As it did now.

She decided to take a bath. She usually took her bath in the morning; at night it tended to keep her awake. But now the hot water relaxed her; the pine odor of the bath oil made her think of a mountain valley just below the timberline. She soaked for a long time, then dried herself and put on a fresh nightgown.

She entered the bedroom and there was Anton, lying on his bed, dressed, his shoes still on. His dirty shoes on her immaculate spread. He must have come in while she was having her bath; she hadn't heard him. A glass had slipped from his hand. She could see the stain the liquid had made on the new yellow rug. Still wet. She ran into the bathroom, got a washcloth, wiped it vigorously. Would it leave a spot? A prescription bottle was standing on the table beside the bed, open. Sleeping pills. Hers. He never took any. His mouth hung open in an agonized way, his breathing was loud. Well, he had taken care of himself. They needn't worry about him.

Graham's call came through at one-fifteen. She said, "He's taken something to sleep. No . . . he won't wake up until morning. I'm sure he won't."

She unlocked the front door. She wrote out the combination of the safe, put it in her purse, and stood the bag on a small table in the library, under a small lamp, which she left on. Then she helped herself to a sleeping pill, and after a little while, a second one. She didn't want to be witness to what was going to happen.

11

Anton Zeller awoke, and by the light filtering through the half-open window he could tell that it was early morning. His head felt heavy, his mouth was dry, and his tongue was rough, like the fur of an animal. For a few seconds his awareness of what had happened was dulled. Then, all at once, recollections seized him, his stomach tightened—Lisa!

He reached for the phone beside his bed, dialed, and got the direct line to Buerkli.

"Barely alive. But she made it through the night, and that's something . . . *of course* she's having transfusions."

"I'll be right over," he said, and added, as if he could order Buerkli around, "For God's sake, save her!"

Fully awake now, he suddenly became aware that the bed next to him was not empty. Helene was an extremely early riser, usually the first up. He had no real idea what she was doing in those early morning hours. Playing golf possibly.

He looked at her curiously. She was lying on her back, her hands folded like a dead person's. It bothered him.

"Helene."

She didn't answer. Normally she'd wake at the slightest sound. Maybe she'd taken too many of her sleeping pills. He reached over, tried to find her pulse, but couldn't. He rose to examine her. Her head lolled awkwardly. Her neck had been broken. A blow to the second cervical vertebra. She was dead.

72

He felt no grief, only a vast astonishment. He had disliked her intensely for such a long time, yet habit was evidently a strong influence. They had lived together for seventeen years, and he had never wished her dead. He went to their dressing room. It was in a state of chaos—the drawers pulled out, tipped over, their contents emptied on the floor. The closets were in the same condition, their clothes piled in a heap on the carpet, the new yellow carpet she had had installed the week before. In his study the door to the safe stood open. Her jewelry was gone, also the cash he kept for emergencies. Thank God he had removed his files on AZ 900 a few weeks ago, when she had begun to behave so hysterically. He crossed the hall to the library. It, too, had been ransacked. In the living room the television set was gone, so was the radio and a treasured antique clock of Helene's. In the kitchen an empty beer bottle stood on the chopping block Mrs. Tummler used for pounding and cutting up the meat. Where was she anyway? Not in her room. Two large suitcases, locked, and some books bound with a leather strap, lay neatly piled on top of each other on the bed, which had been stripped. He went back into the bedroom and stared down at Helene.

Death didn't shock him. He had seen too many people dead. What shocked him was that he had lain in the bed next to hers too drunk to hear what was happening. A feeling of guilt crushed him like a collapsing wall. He sat down on his bed and stared at her still body. He couldn't think clearly. At one moment it seemed to him that he had been justified in drinking himself into a stupor because the woman he loved was fighting for her life; in the next it seemed as if he had killed his wife because he hadn't been alert enough to notice what was going on. He paced the room, but couldn't shake off his daze. Coffee, he thought. It would bring him to his senses.

In the kitchen he found himself automatically putting the kettle on the stove, opening cupboards, measuring out the coffee into the Melitta cup. Helene had been murdered. His mind shied away from the word, so he said it aloud, "Murdered." Why? By whom?

He poured the boiling water over the coffee, watched it settle. It occurred to him that Helene had parents. Faraway strangers. They would have to be notified. And there were other formalities. Stadelmann. He must call his lawyer. Then suddenly he knew what had to be done before anything else. He forgot about the coffee. He turned to the kitchen phone and called the police.

"Professor Zeller speaking. Zeller. Anton Zeller. Krönleinstrasse. I want to report a robbery, and," he hesitated, "a murder."

He drank the coffee, then walked back into the library and poured himself a drink. Closing the mirrored doors of the cupboard, he became aware that he was fully dressed. His suit rumpled, his tie loose, his shirt collar open. It didn't occur to him to tidy himself; instead he looked at his watch. Almost eight-thirty. He was due at the hospital. He dialed the number, asked the senior resident to take over for him, called Buerkli to inquire again about Lisa.

"No change. Don't drive yourself crazy, Anton. We're doing all we can. Take it easy."

He didn't mention that his wife was dead, but held on to the receiver long after Buerkli had hung up. The police arrived a few minutes later. Four men, three of them in uniform, one from homicide—an Inspector Wieland.

They went through the whole apartment, making notes in little books and on large sheets of yellow paper. The inspector wrote in hieroglyphics—shorthand. He commiserated with Zeller about his wife's untimely death, then sat down on a chair opposite the couch. "Sorry, Herr Professor, but I'm going to have to ask you a few questions."

"Go ahead. Can I get you a cup of coffee?"

"Thanks. I've just had breakfast. Now, what time did you come home last night?"

"Can't remember. I was very upset; I got drunk. It may have been any time after twelve. I'm not trying to be difficult. I simply can't recall what time it was."

"Can you remember if you used your key, or was the door unlocked?"

"No, I can't."

"We found the lock wasn't picked."

"Strange. My wife was alone and always afraid of burglars. Quite often she'd put the chain on."

"The front door was not chained and the lock wasn't

picked. Did you leave the door open? I mean, when you came in."

"I don't remember a thing. I may have."

"When did you last see your wife alive?"

"In the late afternoon."

"Where did you go in the late afternoon?"

"To my office."

"It's at the hospital, isn't it?"

"Yes."

"Did you operate?"

"No. I operate in the mornings, in the afternoon only in emergencies. I went to see my patients."

"I see. You had a housekeeper, a Mrs. Tummler. Was she here when you left?"

"I think so."

"She isn't here now?"

"No, she isn't."

"Where does she live?"

"She lived with us, except for weekends, when she went home. I don't know why she isn't here now."

"Have you any idea why anyone, hm . . . should want to kill Mrs. Zeller?"

"Kill her? Of course not. As far as I know she had no enemies."

"Well, what is your opinion about this whole, hm . . . thing?"

"Robbery. Obviously. Her jewelry's gone, so is our cash. About ten thousand francs."

"You keep that much at home?"

"In the safe. Why not? And some other items are missing."

"What items?"

"The television set, the radio, an ormolu clock by Du Tertre; there may be more. My study's been ransacked."

"The safe shows no signs of having been broken into. Seems to have been opened normally, with the combination. You didn't open it, did you?"

Zeller shook his head. "Certainly not. That I'm sure I would remember. I had no reason to open it."

"And your wife?"

"Leave it open? Hardly. Look, inspector, this was obviously robbery. I was too dead to the world to hear

75

them, but my wife evidently did and must have interrupted them. I don't think they had any intention of killing her. They drugged her . . ."

"Why do you always say 'they'? You have come to the conclusion that it was more than one person?"

"Somehow, yes. I don't know why."

"I see. And you were both asleep when entry was made?"

"I can only say I was. Look at my suit. I must have thrown myself on the bed, fully dressed, when I came home."

"And you didn't hear anything?"

"Not a thing."

"Where was the Frau Professor when you came home?"

"I don't know."

"You don't know?"

"Do you always know where your wife is when you get home?"

"Thank God, yes. Right where I expect her to be."

"Well, ours wasn't that kind of a relationship. We were very independent of each other. My profession . . ."

The inspector was staring at Zeller's hands. "Your hands are very strong, aren't they?"

"Yes, they are. Strong and sure. Why?"

"Never mind. May I use the phone?"

"Of course."

For the first time Zeller noticed that the inspector had a mustache. He also wore glasses that hid his eyes. To his surprise the man left the library to phone. Zeller could hear him walk into the bedroom and close the door. He talked for quite a while. When he finally came back, his shoulders were hunched apologetically. "I just talked to my superior. He'll be here in a little while." But it was almost an hour before there was a ring at the door and the mustached inspector got up. "Excuse me, I'll get it."

Zeller was left alone for at least half an hour. It didn't bother him. He went into the bathroom, undressed, showered, dressed, but when he came out he found himself stopped by a man he'd never seen before, a gray-haired man who, like the inspector, wore spectacles, rimless ones. He kept his head low, as if searching for something on the floor. After introducing himself as Inspector Graubart,

76

chief of homicide, he said, "I'm sure everything will be cleared up to your satisfaction, Herr Professor, but for the moment I'm afraid you're going to have to come along with us."

"Where to? I'm overdue at the hospital."

"We know. But right now that's impossible. You see, there'll have to be some further questioning . . ."

"Well, question me, for heaven's sake, and get it over with."

Inspector Graubart shook his head. "I wish I could. Believe me, I hate to inconvenience you, but some things have to move procedurally. I'm sure you understand."

"I want to call my lawyer."

"Certainly. And I shall notify the hospital that you won't be in today."

Zeller spoke to Stadelmann, the words rushing almost incoherently from his mouth. "No, I can't explain it because I don't understand it myself. Nothing makes sense. They say I have to go with them for further questioning . . . who? Homicide. Will you please come to the Badenerstrasse as soon as you can? It's all a crazy mistake."

12

District Attorney Guido Zbinden was looking forward to seeing the suspect, but he was damned if he wasn't going to make him wait a while. Anton Zeller hated to wait; this Zbinden remembered well. "The Tortoise" Anton had called him when they had attended the Collegio Di Papi in Ascona together. He had been short, prone to sickness, and could therefore not run as fast, or catch a ball as well, or participate in so many of the sports at which Anton Zeller excelled.

This childhood envy of Zeller had carried over into Zbinden's adult life. Somehow he had never been able to achieve the appointment of Public Prosecutor, nor was he sufficiently secure financially to open a private practice. And there were other things he resented. Zeller always managed to get away with everything—unconventional behavior, women. Zbinden's wife, Magrit, who had played bridge with poor Helene, had told him all about it, and what Magrit said was gospel. She wouldn't have stood for the things Zeller did; she would leave her husband if she were to find out that there was another woman in his life.

He allowed himself fifteen minutes before entering the chamber. Stadelmann was there, of course. Andreas Stadelmann. Same caliber as Zeller, but he was a bachelor; his transgressions didn't offend the holy state of matrimony. The only things Zbinden held against Stadelmann was that he ate too much, and with too much pleasure, and didn't seem to worry about being overweight,

78

which at his age should be worrying him. Nor did he let weight or age interfere with another passion—beside food and women—namely skiing, which he went in for with zest and extraordinary skill. Seeing him schussing down a slope like a blimp on skis was a popular sight. At the moment, Stadelmann looked ill at ease. Zbinden knew he had had very little time to interview his client, and this pleased him. Stadelmann liked to be well prepared. Zbinden could have scheduled the hearing for later in the afternoon but had chosen not to do so.

"*Gruetzi,* Guido," said Zeller, who had just been brought up from his cell.

Zbinden saw Stadelmann lean forward and whisper something to his client which made him laugh, after which Zeller said, with ironic respect, "Your Honor, what is all this about? I'm being treated like a criminal. Has everybody gone out of their minds?"

Zbinden leafed through the file in front of him. Without looking up, he said. "You are under suspicion of having murdered your wife, Helene Reynolds Zeller." He read the name aloud slowly, as if he had never heard it before.

Zeller jumped to his feet. "I did not murder my wife," he shouted.

Stadelmann forced him down again while Zbinden, ignoring the interruption, sat back in a leisurely fashion and went on with the questioning. "Is it true that you came home last night drunk?"

"Dead drunk and exhausted."

"At what time?"

"As I have already told the police, I have no idea what time."

"Is it true that you did not see the deceased when you got home, or make any attempt to find out where she was?"

"I fell on the bed, I didn't even undress, and slept immediately."

"Is it true that you spent most of the time previous to your coming home at the Kantonspital, in the room of a certain Lisa Tanner?"

"Objection," from Stadelmann. "I would like the question rephrased." But to Zbinden's surprise, Zeller didn't seem to mind the insinuation or wait for the ruling on the objection.

"She was very badly injured by the attack of a madman and was on the critical list."

"Would you please describe in what position you found yourself and your wife when you awoke?"

Hurriedly Zeller repeated what he had told the police.

"I would like to point out," said Stadelmann, "that it was Professor Zeller himself who called the police to report the murder."

"He also reported a robbery." And to Zeller, "Why did you decide it was a robbery?"

"Well, that was obvious. As I've already said—the place was a wreck, several valuable things were missing . . ."

"What things?"

"My wife's jewelry. Cash. The television set, a valuable clock, a Du Tertre."

"What made you think of murder?"

"Her neck was broken . . . but I've already described the whole thing to the police, in detail."

"Read it back," Zbinden directed the officer who was taking notes. He looked, Zeller thought, like a freshly baked Swiss roll, which made him suddenly feel hungry, but the man's monotonous voice retelling the whole grim story soon dispelled that.

"Obviously robbery," said Stadelmann, when the man got through. "Mrs. Zeller's jewelry was extremely valuable."

"But Mrs. Zeller is dead." Zbinden stretched the last word as if it were an elastic he was playing with. "There is a difference between robbery and murder."

"I'm aware of that," said Zeller. "In my opinion she must have heard something that wakened her, and got up, and interrupted whatever was going on, and to keep her quiet they killed her."

"You seem to see it all very clearly."

"Well, you give me a better theory."

Stadelmann shook his head. Zbinden looked furious. "I am not here," he said, "to theorize on what may or may not have happened. One thing seems to be certain—somebody made it very easy for whoever did it. The lock on the front door wasn't picked, and the safe was apparently opened with the combination. And there are no strange fingerprints to be found anywhere. Did you hear any argument between these supposed thieves and your wife?"

"I did not. I slept like a log until I woke up to find my wife dead."

"Had you taken any drugs before you went to sleep?"

"I never do. Never have to. No . . . wait a minute—I did take one of her pills that night. Now I remember. Maybe two. That, on top of the alcohol must have done it. Only goes to show what a state I was in. And what a horse I am. Barbiturates and alcohol should *not* be mixed."

"I wish you would tell your story more chronologically," said Zbinden. "It would be more convincing."

This irritated Zeller. "The situation is a mess. I'm telling it as best I can. I find it hard to piece together."

"You said 'one of her pills.' She took sleeping pills?"

"Yes."

"Why?"

"Really, Guido . . . your Honor . . . because she slept badly."

"Why did she sleep badly?"

Zeller shrugged. "In everybody's lifetime there's a period of nervousness, restlessness, insomnia."

"And you would say that her nervousness, restlessness, and insomnia had nothing to do with your wanting to get rid of her?"

"Get rid of her? What an extraordinary way to put it."

"That's how Mrs. Zeller put it." He pointed to a red leather-bound book on the desk in front of him. "Her diary."

It was strange to think that Helene had kept a diary, like a schoolgirl. "I wanted her to give me a divorce, if that's what you mean."

"Not entirely. Did you ask her for a divorce?"

"Several times."

"You wanted a divorce to marry Miss Lisa Tanner, your surgical nurse?"

"Leave her out of it!" Zeller, suddenly beside himself, was shouting again.

"But you were insisting on a divorce."

"Yes."

"To marry another woman?"

"Eventually, yes."

Zbinden rarely encountered such honesty. He saw Stadelmann's desperation and for the first time in his life felt sympathy for his once hated schoolmate.

Stadelmann frowned. Didn't Zeller see that from the police's point of view he could have done the job himself? On the missing cash they had only his word, the jewelry he could have hidden or thrown away, the few other objects could have been gotten rid of earlier, Mrs. Tummler's convenient disappearance on the very day—above all, the unpicked lock and the safe opened without force. It must appear to anybody that he was trying to make it look like a burglary to cover himself.

"Your housekeeper, Mrs. Tummler," Zbinden went on, "in your opinion could she possibly have had anything to do with what took place?"

"Hedwig Tummler?" Zeller's mystification was reflected in his voice. He was evidently finding it difficult to focus his mind on anything as trivial as his unobtrusive housekeeper. "Good heavens, no. Whatever made you ask that?"

"She had packed her things the day all this happened. Did you fire her?"

"Why should I have fired her? She suited me fine. Thoughtful, efficient, intelligent, and knew her place. I always thought Helene was pleased with her too. Of course, I really can't tell. I was so upset that afternoon, my memory of it is vague. I might have done anything."

"Anything?"

"Anything except kill a human being." Zeller's voice was angry again. "I'm a doctor, Guido. My profession is to save life, not destroy it."

"That's something you're going to have to prove." Their eyes met during a brief silence, a silence that was almost audible. "I shall have to detain you for further hearings."

"Detain me?"

"In other words, Professor Zeller, you are under arrest."

Zeller paled, but only for a moment, then he reddened with rage. He turned to Stadelmann. "The man's mad. For God's sake, Andreas, ask for bail."

"There is no bail for suspicion of murder," said Stadelmann.

13

"We are dissatisfied," said the man with the crutches, knocking one of them so hard against the table that a waitress came hurrying over.

"Anything wrong, *mein Herr?*"

"No, no. Everything's fine."

Except my situation, thought Graham Foley. He had been summoned to meet his employer here, at the Restaurant Mövenpick on the Paradeplatz, one of several Mövenpicks scattered all over Zurich. For a chain restaurant the food was surprisingly good.

The man with the crutches, whose face never showed any expression, shoved his Birchermuesli aside. He seemed to have lost his appetite for the concoction of oatmeal soaked in cream and fresh fruit.

"You haven't produced anything."

Graham's stomach tightened. It hadn't been right since he had discovered that his laborious efforts to court Helene had been in vain. My ulcers will kill me, he thought, before Smith, Schmitt, Schmidt gets around to it.

"And on top of this, you've got our man in jail."

"That's not my fault."

"We happen to disagree. We can't remember having given orders to kill anybody."

"I didn't kill her."

"So she committed suicide? The police don't see it that way."

"You should be glad she's dead." Graham's lips were

trembling. "Alive she'd have been a bloody nuisance. She could have identified me. She was that kind of woman, couldn't make up her mind. She might have confessed everything to her husband. I think it's a good thing she's dead and we don't have to worry about the unpredictable behavior of a nymphomaniac."

"We?" said his employer. "I'm not in trouble, you are. Whatever made you think that what we were after was in the safe in their apartment?"

"She told me it was. And it wasn't all that simple to get her to the point where she was willing to give me the combination."

"We can skip that. No longer interesting. As I said before, you're in trouble."

Graham Foley needed a lift. He ordered another carafe of wine. The lift, though, wasn't forthcoming.

"Bad trouble," the man with the crutches went on. "Unless . . ."

There was a calculated pause to let the word take effect, and Graham's expected response came promptly, "Unless?"

"Unless you get him out of jail."

"Out of jail? Good God, that's impossible!"

"Nothing is impossible if properly handled. People have escaped from more strictly guarded prisons, as for instance Regensdorf. The jail in the Badenerstrasse seems to us to pose less of a problem. You've made connections with all sorts of people; use them."

Yes, thought Graham, I will.

His dread of Smith was subsiding. For all his shrewdness, Smith apparently had no idea that Graham had joined forces against him with someone possibly more powerful. Suddenly he felt pleased, almost superior to the man who had been making life hell for him for years. Beaulieu and he would work out something; they'd get this bloody doctor out of jail. But it's not you who will profit by it, he thought, looking Smith in the eye, something he'd never done before.

Smith didn't notice, or chose not to notice, the change. "Since you seem too incompetent to manage alone," he went on, "somebody will be watching over you. Whatever

84

help you may need in the escape, apply for it." He gave Graham a telephone number. "Memorize it."

"What's the name?"

"You don't need a name. Only the right person will answer. Pick up your passport at the usual place. And now, a final item: where is her jewelry?"

Graham Foley nodded in the direction of the Schweizerkreditanstalt on the opposite side of the Paradeplatz. "In my safe-deposit box."

"Get it."

"Now?"

"Now. We'll be waiting outside in a taxi. Get us one on your way out."

Cruising taxis were a rarity in Zurich. Graham phoned for one from the restaurant, gave the name of the bank. "In fifteen minutes."

He crossed the Paradeplatz. The streetcars and automobiles converging at high speed from every side were a hazard he'd learned to cope with. Today he didn't wait for the light to change, but made a suicidal dash to the huge building on the other side. Helene's jewelry was worth a small fortune. The bank probably had several exits, but he'd never get away with escape. Not at this point. They'd track him down. He shouldn't have waited so long; he should have made his getaway the moment he had realized Zeller's files were not in the safe.

He rang the bell that opened the gate to the vault, signed, produced his key. A man took the key, opened the gate to the deposit boxes, row upon row, and came out with a long rectangular box. "Want a private room?"

It took less than a minute to remove the gray leather bag. "That's all," Graham told the attendant as he gave back box and key. It was. Beaulieu had pocketed the cash they had found in the safe. Those ten thousand francs would never get Graham free. His only chance of a future went with the jewelry, which Beaulieu had so correctly decided would have to go to Smith. . . . "Or you're in trouble." Trouble? The understatement had made his grin look sick.

Inside the taxi, Smith pocketed the little gray bag and told the driver, "Kloten."

The airport. "You're leaving?"

"That's our plan."

"And where can I reach you?"

"No need to reach me. You have the only number you need."

"How much time are you giving me?"

"A month. To the day. After that, you're dead."

14

Lisa remained on the critical list for ten days. On the morning of the eleventh, she suddenly rallied. She opened her eyes slowly, making an enormous effort to lift what seemed a heavy weight on her lids. At first she didn't know where she was, then gradually she recalled what had happened and began to tremble uncontrollably.

"Be calm," said a soft voice. "Everything's all right."

In a chair, in the left corner of the room, sat a man. Vaguely she remembered having seen him before. A rather elegantly dressed man whose slim body consisted more of legs than anything else. He let the paper he'd been reading slide from his hands. "Everything's all right," he repeated.

She was too weak to ask what he was doing in her room, a hospital room, she realized, white-walled, the windows half-open, the curtains trembling softly. Flowers and get-well cards were arranged neatly in a rack on the wall opposite her.

Professor Buerkli and a nurse came in. Buerkli gestured to the man, and waited for him to leave. He started to examine Lisa. She was asked to breathe deeply and nearly passed out. "I'm dizzy," she managed to say apologetically.

"But I think we're over the worst," he told her. "You're a lucky girl. We had to remove the spleen, and after our repair work on the lung, you weren't in too good shape for it."

Briefly he sketched in the extent of her injuries and what had been done for her. "And now be a good girl, keep as quiet as you can and try to build up your strength. You've lost a lot of weight. And don't talk too much, above all, don't tire yourself."

Lisa was glad to lie back. Suddenly she could remember being turned and turned again when she had tried to change her position. She thanked God that Buerkli had been the one to take care of her.

The strange man came back the next day. He picked up his newspaper and sat down in the chair he had occupied the day before. "Who are you?" she asked. "I seem to remember having seen . . ."

He put a finger to his finely chiseled mouth, an Adonis mouth, she thought, altogether an Adonis type. "Don't talk. Doctor's orders."

He began to read, turning the pages soundlessly. Lisa closed her eyes, and the scene of the night she had been attacked came back to her. She screamed. A nurse rushed in. "What's wrong? Are you in pain?"

Lisa began to cry. Professor Buerkli came and held her hand. "You've been through a lot, child," he said. "But you must try to put what happened out of your mind. Think of other things." And with a gesture of his head in the direction of the strange man, "Let him entertain you. He's an amusing fellow and seems devoted to you. In a week or two we'll let you go, but if you don't do your best, it's going to take longer and my reputation will be ruined. And you don't want that, do you?"

He stroked her hand. It made her think of Toni. Where was he? She would have liked to ask Buerkli, but felt embarrassed and kept silent. Around lunchtime Regina came in, still wearing her OR cap. She knelt beside Lisa's bed because she didn't want her friend to have to look up at her towering height. Again the man left the room.

"Who is he?"

"He saved your life."

"He saved my life?"

"He fought off the man who nearly did you in, then he helped me get you here."

"But why?"

"I have no idea. But he's a very nice fellow. I told Professor Buerkli that you would have been dead without him, so he has let him stay here. He's been with you every day. He's brought you flowers, he always brings the nurses something. They adore him. His name is Gustave Beaulieu."

"I want Toni. Where is he?"

"He was here every moment he could spare, but you were out like a light, for very near a week. Yesterday he was called, a case in Madrid. I'm sure he'll phone in today. He does every day."

"Tell them to connect me."

"Oh, no," said Regina. "You're not talking on any phone yet. But I'll take a message."

"Tell him I love him."

"I could have figured that out by myself," said Regina, and left as quickly as she could.

When the man with the French name returned, Lisa asked him, "Why have you been sitting here and bringing me flowers? Schwester Regina tells me you saved my life."

"I happened to be there. You see, I moved into your apartment house a few days before it happened. I heard the commotion . . ."

"Did you see him?"

"Not well enough to give a satisfactory description to the police."

"I didn't either. I was barely able to talk when they started questioning me, and all confused about what had taken place. And today I still can't see it any more clearly. They haven't found him, have they?"

"Not yet."

"What could he have been after. You took the envelope from him, didn't you?"

"Yes. And I have it with me. Would you like it now?"

"Please."

He got up, took the manila envelope out of his attaché case and put it on her night table.

"In the drawer, please."

He put it in the drawer.

"But why are you doing all this for me?" she wanted to know. "It's way beyond the call of duty, isn't it?"

"I suppose any able-bodied man would have done what

I did, but the rest . . . I'm sure it sounds foolish, incredible even, but when I saw you there, lying on the floor, it was, well . . . I am forty years old, and that is a suspicious age to fall in love with a girl for the first time."

Just as Toni had found her. What was it about that peculiar position that attracted men? She looked at him again. Was he homosexual? There was something effeminate about the way he sat and moved, and his soft, white hands.

"I couldn't believe it at first," he went on. "I thought, Gustave, *mon vieux*, you're balmy. Then I came up here to see you, and your crazy American friend almost threw me out. After he heard how helpful I'd been he had to shut up. Not that it came easy to him. And there you were, so pale, so still, like the mask I have at home. You must know it, everybody does—*L'Inconnue de la Seine*. It was all the rage in my mother's day, and I've never stopped liking it. Perhaps I was in love with it. So sad, so serene, and you looked just like her."

Chris came. He had come every afternoon after office hours. "Can't we shake that guy?" he said petulantly, just after Beaulieu had left. "I hate to sit at my desk and think of him mooning at you. He's interfering with my work. I know he saved your life, but any able-bodied man . . ."

"He just finished saying that," said Lisa, smiling. "Calm down, darling. He doesn't bother me, and he doesn't stay long. He's sort of comforting. Anyway, when he's here I can keep the horrors off my mind. And he brings the nurses candy from Sprüngli."

"I can bring the nurses candy from Sprüngli."

"He thinks he's in love with me."

"I'm in love with you, but I don't have time to sit here for hours on end."

"I know. You have to fill out papers, listen to complaints, give orders to the passport division, help stranded Americans to get home when they run out of money or their charter flights are canceled . . ." She stopped herself as she realized that she was repeating the very things Toni had said about Chris, ending up with, "What a job for a man. *No thank you!*"

"Well, doesn't he have anything to do?" asked Chris. "What does the man live on?"

"I'll try to remember to ask him next time," said Lisa.

"Forget it. Let's talk about you. I'm planning to take you away just as soon as they let you out of here. I've just consulted Buerkli and he thinks in two weeks . . . so now I can put in for my vacation. Davos or St. Moritz, I thought, but he seems to favor somewhere farther south. I'll make inquiries."

"You're sweet," said Lisa, "and I'm fond of you, very fond of you, but Chris, I don't love you. I've been thinking about it the last few days and before . . . before all this happened. You shouldn't spend your vacation with me. I told you you should find another girl."

"And I've told you that I've tried to. But by now I know I'll die a crotchety old bachelor if you don't marry me."

"Oh Chris, don't make me feel so guilty."

"Chacun à son désastre," he said, and laughed.

That evening, just before she went off duty, Sister Clara came in. She should have looked in long before this, if only out of courtesy, but she hadn't felt equal to participating in the foolish deception the others were practicing. It couldn't be kept from the girl forever that her lover had murdered his wife, so what were they waiting for?

She might possibly have been pretty in her youth, Lisa thought, as the woman walked up to her bed, but today she looked like an apple that had dropped from the tree before it was ripe and lain on the ground, exposed to the sun and rain. And to ants. Which was a mean thought, because Sister Clara's face had been scarred by acne. Not her fault. In her street clothes, which were dowdy, she looked plainer than ever.

"We're glad to see you getting better every day," she said. "Everybody was worried about you."

Sister Clara saw that Lisa's chestnut brown hair had lost none of its sparkle, her fine features and delicate bone structure seemed even more pronounced by her pallor, and the curve of her mouth reminded her of a rose petal. No question, Tanner was the type whose frailty made her more appealing, and she, Sister Clara, had no appealing quality.

She had considered sometimes having her face lifted, but had always decided against it in the end. She was afraid of pain, and of being laughed at for such hopeless vanity. Besides, it cost money. In a psychology class she had been taught that those who had to live without love poured their affection into money, and it was true of her —she saved every penny she could. In the end her little nest egg might even attract a man.

"What are you planning to do from here?" she asked.

"Rest. What else? As long as I can."

"Will you go to Ruvigliana? I was there two years ago. The food is good."

Lisa had once visited a colleague at that convalescent home. "I'd like to go somewhere more bracing," she said. "And on my own."

"Can you afford to?"

"I think so."

"Well," was all Sister Clara said, but she was thinking that loose living apparently resulted in greater affluence than did her own narrow path of rectitude.

The telephone rang, and Lisa moved so hastily to answer it, she almost knocked over the water carafe on her bedside table. "Hello." And then, obviously crestfallen, a short conversation with Regina.

She lay back, all elation wiped from her face, nothing on her mind but the wish that Sister Clara would leave her alone.

"You're going to be disappointed many times," said Sister Clara, "if you're expecting Professor Zeller to call." She paused. "I think the whole thing's idiotic. You're not a child. Someday you've got to find out . . ."

Suddenly Lisa felt cold. "Find out what?" She drew the blanket up to her chin. "I'll see him just as soon as he gets back from Madrid."

"Madrid? He's not in Madrid."

Lisa swallowed—an act she suddenly found very difficult —and said, "Will you please tell me what you're driving at?"

"Professor Zeller has been arrested for murder."

She couldn't have heard right. She was having a nightmare, a bizarre dream. "You're trying to tell me . . ."

"He killed his wife. The night after you were attacked. While she was sleeping. *Finis*. The place was ransacked; her jewelry was gone. The general impression though is that he staged the whole thing. They feel he doesn't have a chance."

Lisa found her voice at last. "I don't believe a word you're saying, and neither do you."

"Well, read all about it yourself and form your own opinion. I saved the clippings for you." She took them out of her large black bag and tossed them on the bed. "I thought you'd better read them lying down." Lisa was trying desperately not to reach out for the papers. "Would you like a glass of water?" Sister Clara filled Lisa's glass from the carafe. Lisa paid no attention to her. She was staring at the headline: "RENOWNED HEART SURGEON ARRESTED FOR MURDER."

"Sorry," said Sister Clara, "but I thought you'd better know and not be waiting vainly for him to turn up. Get it over with, as I always say."

Lisa didn't notice Sister Clara leaving. She began to read.

15

As soon as she felt strong enough, Lisa went to see Zeller. While still in the hospital, she had filed for permission. It was granted only once a week, a quarter of an hour. Chris drove her to the jail. Traffic was heavy, still they were early. An expanse of vine, partially overgrowing the building, made it look less formidable. Chris circled the block. He passed a small square with thick chestnut trees and cement pots overflowing with geraniums, pink and red. The pale blue dial of St. Jacob's Church looked down on a predominantly poor neighborhood, in so far as one could call any area of Zurich poor. A policeman, in the orange phosphorescent coat he wore to be clearly visible in fog and rain, was directing traffic. There were so many entrances, even Chris was confused. "Just stop anywhere," she said, "and don't wait. I'm quite able to find my way alone, and I'll take a taxi back."

After asking her way, she found the right entrance in the Rotwandstrasse, a small door cut into a huge iron gate. It led into a courtyard that was flanked on three sides by office buildings, a parking lot for the district attorney's staff, a small stretch of lawn, some flowers even here. On the fourth side, the windows were barred, astonishingly large windows for what she realized had to be cells.

She rang the bell beside the gray, arched door. When it was finally opened by a pleasant old man, she walked through another iron gate, which he unlocked for her, into a small patio. Two large trees, a few bicycles unchained under a slanting roof, a woolen blanket at the far end, airing over a carpet-beating rack. When she finally entered the prison itself, the almost antiseptic cleanliness amazed her. Not a scrap of litter anywhere, no graffiti, not a trace of dust on radiators or sills. The visiting rooms were occupied. In the waiting room the modern chairs were comfortable, the round tabletop shone as if never used, the floors here as everywhere were waxed to nearly perfect reflection. The whole place looked strangely unused, and it was quiet. The few people passing by—visiting relatives, perhaps a psychiatrist or lawyer, a priest— moved silently. If they spoke at all, it was, from where she sat, inaudible. At last she was ushered into one of the small visiting rooms. Zeller entered through a door on the opposite side, behind him a guard who sat down on a chair against the wall facing her, an arm's length away from the prisoner. All that separated her from Zeller was a narrow table across which one could hold hands.

She couldn't imagine why she had thought he would be dressed like a convict when the trial hadn't come up yet and he hadn't been convicted, but she had visualized him in prison garb, and it was somehow reassuring to see him in his ordinary clothes. Yet it made the whole situation even more unreal.

"Toni."

He didn't look as bad as she had expected, just terribly nervous. Every now and then a slight tic below the right eye, and he was pale.

"Thank God you've come."

He wanted to hear every detail about the progress of her illness and recovery. "On top of everything else I nearly went mad worrying over you. Stadelmann did his best to reassure me, I've seen him almost daily, but I wanted to see for myself. You look terribly frail. Well, no wonder. It's a miracle . . . we should be thanking God that you're here at all. You're going to take Buerkli's advice, aren't you? And go away for a while?" But from his tone and the anxiety on his face, she knew it was the last thing he wanted.

"I couldn't go away now with you here. I couldn't bear it."

A flicker of relief passed across his harassed face, but it

was quickly gone. "There's nothing you can do for me."

"I can be close. And now I want to know all about you. How are you? How do you feel?" And then, because she knew how much he loved solitude, "Are you . . . are you in with others, or are you alone?"

"I have a single cell."

"What . . ." Lisa hesitated. "What's it like?"

"Small. Let's not waste time talking about it."

"But I want to be able to imagine you."

"An iron bedstead," he said, his voice suddenly bitter, "a locker, a table, fastened to the wall, a bench, fastened to the floor, nothing standing loose, nothing a prisoner might pick up and use to attack somebody. A toilet. A washbowl in the corner, screened off, and all this splendor on a shiny parquet floor . . ." He shook his head.

"Are you allowed to read?"

"Yes. Books from the library. Innocuous stuff. But I get my medical journals, and I can put in for medical books."

"And the food?"

"Edible."

"May I bring you something special?"

He shook his head. "Not allowed. Here everybody's equal, rich and poor, sane and insane."

"Do you mix with the others?"

"Rarely, thank God. Three or four times a week we're taken out for exercise, but we're not allowed to speak."

"How are the guards?"

"Human. Reasonable. So is the director. The superintendent is a nice fellow."

"You look as if you've lost weight." She placed her hands over his across the narrow table. Strange how anxiety could kill all sensuousness. She knew he felt the same way. At this moment they could only be solace to each other.

"When will the trial come up?"

He shrugged; suddenly he looked desperate. "Three months, six months, nine months—how do I know? Zbinden got an extension."

Realizing what conviction would mean to him, she had to ask, "Toni, you didn't . . ."

He saw her anguish. "I didn't do it."

"I know," she said. "I never doubted it. But then I

know you. What do you think your chances are of convincing a jury?"

"I'd better convince them," he said. "I have no intention of accepting a life sentence or sitting out an appeal. I wonder sometimes if I'll be able to stick it out here until I'm let go." His eyes narrowed; he looked as if he meant what he was saying. "There's got to be a dismissal or I'll kill myself."

The guard raised two fingers, like a man monitoring a broadcast. "Time's up," he said, and rose from his chair. Lisa looked at him imploringly. He sat down again.

"Toni," she said, "don't talk like that, don't let yourself think along those lines."

"You haven't been here for four weeks. You haven't sat through hearings that get more and more nightmarish, and tried to stay sane. I can't take it, Lisa. I've never been able to take it. My father punished me once, kept me in my room for three days. If he hadn't locked me in, perhaps as a point of honor, I'd have endured it. Besides, I'd really committed what in his eyes was a crime, fooled around with his instruments. But he locked me in. I ran my head against the door until my nose bled; I yelled so loudly, people gathered in the street outside the house; in the end I jumped out of the window. Broke my arm. My father said, 'I see you're not only going to have to be punished, you're going to have to learn to take punishment.' I never did. I realize that now. But this isn't punishment! *This is injustice!*"

"Toni, they've got nothing but circumstantial evidence."

"You've been talking to Stadelmann." He shook his head. "No five years for me. I tell you, I don't think I'm going to be able to stick it out to the trial. I can't be locked up! I'm going out of my mind."

The guard cut in. "You've got to go, Miss."

"Is there anything you want, anything I can bring you, send you?"

"Freedom."

"I'll do my best."

He got up, followed the guard out, was gone. Lisa sat on in the empty room until the door was opened for the next visitor. Her best. What could she do? How could she possibly help him?

16

The building on Talackerstrasse where the American consulate was located seemed to absorb a whole city block. On all sides, banks, tourist offices, a real estate agency, and inside the offices of Olympic Airways, a hearing aid firm, a cosmetic studio, an interior decorator, dentists, lawyers. A moment before entering, Lisa noticed Chris's car between the trees of the small parking lot that faced the building, a conservative navy blue European Ford that made the little red Peugeot parked beside it look brazen. She hesitated—should she walk up the wide, black marble staircase or take the elevator?—and decided on the latter. Steps still tired her.

She was ushered into Andreas Stadelmann's office after a good ten-minute wait. When she finally entered, she saw she was not to be alone with the lawyer. Christopher Chase rose from one chair, Gustave Beaulieu from another, and a man she hadn't met before got up from an old-fashioned brown leather couch. Stadelmann introduced him. "Inspector Wieland."

He was of a rather rotund build and made you think somehow of a nice new potato. He sat down on the couch again and went on with what he had been doing, fitting pieces into a jigsaw puzzle spread out on a coffee table. "My way of concentrating," he said. "Hope you don't mind."

"Inspector Wieland is head of our investigation bureau," said Stadelmann. "I believe I told you about him."

"And what are you doing here? Chris? Gustave?"

She didn't really object to their presence. Chris she had expected. His proximity, in the same building, frequently brought him down to the lawyer's office. And Gustave? Although a new friend, he seemed to have been a part of her life for a long time, the first man she had ever known to make no physical demands. In spite of his declaration of love, she was sure now that he was homosexual, and grateful for it. At this point she couldn't have responded physically, perhaps not even to Toni. She still felt drained.

"We've been doing a little investigating on our own," said Chris.

"But with little success," Wieland remarked dryly, without looking up from his puzzle.

"I'm not so pessimistic," said Chris. "We know of at least two young men who seem to have had relations with Zeller's wife."

"Relations?" Lisa was stunned. Toni had never mentioned any unfaithfulness on Helene's part, in fact he couldn't possibly have known, or he would have had no problem with a divorce.

"Her diary was quite illuminating," said Stadelmann. "She noted first names and we . . . that is to say Inspector Wieland, tracked them down by asking around the neighborhood. Their jobs were surprisingly menial."

"But none of them will talk," said Chris. "Of course they've been subpoenaed."

"That won't make them talk," said Wieland.

"We can afford to let it cost us something," said Stadelmann. "That may help."

"Whatever you do," said Lisa, finally sitting down in the chair offered her, "hurry. Anything to give him some hope. I saw him yesterday, and he's desperate. He says he'll kill himself if he's convicted, and I believe him."

"If he's convicted," said Stadelmann, "We'll appeal. This can go on for years."

"But *he* can't go on for years. Not like this."

"Unfortunately," said Stadelmann. "Let's face it, this sort of thing can't be hurried. I don't know if you know, but Zbinden has asked for and been granted an extension, and he can do that again and again. New evidence keeps coming in, but most of it is prejudicial. Among other things a police report of a call on June seventh, put in by a neighbor, to the effect that Zeller tried to run over his wife, and when she screamed and roused the whole neighborhood, he struck her."

"It isn't true!" Lisa rose from her chair, but sat down again, feeling utterly helpless. "It was just another one of her hysterical outbursts. She was crouched in his path when he drove out of the garage. He nearly did run over her, but without any intention on his part. And he did slap her, to bring her to her senses. Of course by that time a crowd had gathered." She covered her face with her hands. "How dreadful! How things can be misconstrued!"

"How do you know about all this?"

"He told me. Later they talked it over and she agreed that in three months, if he still wanted a divorce, she would give it to him."

"That could be mitigating," said Stadelmann. "Anyway, I was going to ask you to testify at the next hearing. I hope you feel up to it."

She didn't, but she said, "You know I'd do anything to help."

"And I'm going to swear under oath," said Chris, "that you couldn't possibly have been the motive. You no longer believed Zeller would get a divorce and marry you, and had sent him away because you had decided to marry me. They'll probably ask you to corroborate this."

"Miss Tanner," said Wieland, "do you know anything about a tall young man with whom Mrs. Zeller was seen on several occasions? Recently? It seems they played golf together at the Dolder."

Lisa shook her head. "Nothing."

"He too is mentioned in the diary," said Wieland, "but unfortunately this time we have no lead to the man."

Just then Beaulieu broke in. "If you ask me," he said, "I figure the whole thing differently. I don't see it as a man who murdered his wife to get his freedom."

"What do you figure?" said Lisa.

Beaulieu was sitting opposite Stadelmann, his short-fingered hands, freshly manicured, spread out on the mahogany desk in front of him. When he took them away, they left damp marks on the wood.

"Inspector Wieland and I had a talk." Beaulieu lit one of his French cigarettes, inhaled deeply, coughed.

"About what?" asked Chris, a look of annoyance on his face that almost made Lisa smile. How he resented her gay-friend.

"About Zeller's work to combat AS," said Wieland. "He has this farm in Maur where he keeps all sorts of animals. He injects them regularly with something he prepares in his lab there. We got the men to talk. It wasn't difficult. They are devoted to him and miserable about his situation, so it was easy to persuade them that they could be helpful. Unfortunately neither of them is very bright. However, we did manage to get out of them that he keeps monkeys on a high-cholesterol diet, and after a certain amount of time has passed—neither knew exactly how long—he injects them every three days for weeks, or months—all pretty vague—with a preparation. Of course they have no idea what it is."

He paused, having just found a piece in his puzzle that fitted.

"They also told us," said Beaulieu, addressing Lisa, "that you quite frequently assisted at the Maur lab. What does he get from these freshly slaughtered animals?"

Lisa sat very still, her hands folded in her lap. She couldn't help it, but she felt all the time—whether Stadelmann was addressing her, or Beaulieu, or this inspector, even Chris—as if she were already in the courtroom and had to watch every word. Now she found herself reluctant to reveal anything about Zeller's work. She didn't know why. And it couldn't possibly have anything to do with the case.

"Whatever he happens to need," she said. "He was experimenting. All I did really was hand him the instruments. The rest didn't interest me. You see," and she forced a smile, "it was an opportunity to be together."

"Well," said Beaulieu, "I see the whole thing like this: somebody was after Zeller's research. The break-in at Maur, your room, Lisa, being ransacked, the attack on you . . ."

"Did you know that your room was bugged?" Wieland interrupted.

"My room was bugged? Why on earth . . ."

Helene, she thought. But no. Why should Helene have had a listening device installed when it was no secret that her husband and Lisa were lovers? It wasn't she who was after a divorce.

"And on the same night . . ." Beaulieu again, "or was it the following night? . . . the robbery at Zeller's apartment. I think they took the jewelry and the few other items that were missing as a cover-up for what they were really after." He turned to Lisa again. "Do you happen to know if he kept his files in the safe?"

She hesitated. All eyes were on her. "He used to. But he removed them a few weeks, or maybe it was days, before the robbery. After . . ." Should she go on? But it was too late to turn back. Besides, there apparently *was* a connection, or at least Beaulieu thought there was, between the robbery and Zeller's findings. "After Mrs. Zeller began to behave so hysterically," she finished her sentence.

"You mean he was afraid she might take some sort of revenge with his papers?"

Lisa shrugged. "I don't know. Possibly. He didn't give any reason."

"Well then," said Beaulieu, "I'm sure I'm right. When they didn't find what they were after in the safe, they needed more time. I think the fact that his wife died was an accident; I don't think it was intended. Maybe she came to while they were looking, and they gave her more to put her under again. Too much."

"That's been Zeller's theory all along," said Stadelmann.

"And he's right," said Beaulieu.

"If we can prove it . . ."

"He would go free. Undoubtedly."

"But who could possibly be after his findings?" Lisa wanted to know.

"My dear girl," Beaulieu's smile was almost fatherly, "several drug firms have been after him to sell his invention, as Dr. Stadelmann explained to me the other day."

"So?" Lisa looked puzzled. "What drug company would . . ."

Beaulieu interrupted her. "Some have been known to go to such lengths, and to get away with it and profit by it. Dr. Stadelmann explained to me that Professor Zeller wasn't willing to release his vaccine until he considered it safe. Herr Doktor, we never did finish our conversation. What did he intend to do with it once he considered it safe?"

"He has a friend," said Stadelmann, "an organic chemist who works in a small pharmaceutical factory. Zeller was toying with the idea of buying the factory and, together with this man, processing and manufacturing the vaccine. He has a deep distrust of the drug industry."

"I can't blame him," said Beaulieu.

"Miss Tanner," said Wieland, picking up the part of the puzzle he had finished and placing it carefully in the box, then raking the still unfitted pieces in after it, "do you know the Zeller's housekeeper, Mrs. Tummler?"

Lisa frowned. "No. I saw her once, but that's all."

"Could you describe her?"

"Middle-aged. Gray. Wears her hair in an old-fashioned bun on the top of her head. Plump. A short, strong body and surprisingly slender legs."

"You have a good memory."

"You acquire one as a nurse. You learn to remember faces, voices, the way a person moves."

Wieland pulled a photo out of his vest pocket and showed it to her. She nodded. "That's her."

"Where did you see her?"

"At a concert. Zeller pointed her out. He said he wished I could cook as well."

"Do you know anything about her personal life?"

"Nothing really. I think Zeller mentioned that she liked children. And, oh yes, she's quite a mountain climber. Phenomenal for her age, according to Zeller."

"Well, she has disappeared," said Wieland. "Apparently she left the Zellers on the day of the burglary, which may or may not be significant. Her nephew who lives with her—she has her own apartment, which you may not know—got her things from the Zellers, but he has no idea, or won't tell, where she went."

"Couldn't we put an ad in the paper?"

"We did. No result. She's probably afraid of becoming involved. I have her apartment under surveillance and I've posted a man at the airport. In my opinion Mrs.

Tummler has left the country, but will come back to her apartment once things have begun to blow over."

"I tell you," said Beaulieu, "she's just lying low. I understand she wasn't there the morning Zeller found his wife dead. She slept at the Krönleinstrasse, except over weekends, and it was a Thursday morning, wasn't it? And she wasn't there. Why wasn't she there?"

"The prosecutor will say Zeller sent her away so as to be able to stage the whole thing without her interference."

"Chris!"

"You've got to face reality, Lisa. That's exactly what he'll say. A juicy bit of circumstantial evidence."

"Then it's of the utmost importance that we find Mrs. Tummler. You say she has a nephew. I'll go to see him."

"You'll do nothing of the sort," said Chris. "He's been investigated. They couldn't get anything out of him. He said his aunt had gone away, and he didn't know where she was or when she was coming back. Apparently no shining light."

Wieland picked up his puzzle box. "This has been a fruitful meeting," he said. "And your theory, Mr. Beaulieu, is interesting. I'll give it some thought."

The meeting broke up, and although Beaulieu obviously had no intention of leaving Lisa and Chris alone, Chris managed to shake him off, not very diplomatically.

"How did he get in on all this anyway?" he asked, when they were alone. "Did you ask him to help?"

"No. I imagine he got in touch with Stadelmann on his own."

"I can't stand fags."

"Why? They're often very good company, intelligent, sensitive. Why hate them?"

"When I was ten a teacher tried . . ."

"Oh, come on, Chris. You're grown up and now and can look after yourself." She had to smile. "I'll take care of you. And you should be glad, really. I'm so safe with him."

"What does he do anyway, besides hang around you?"

"He repairs and restores clocks."

"A watchmaker."

"Better than that. He specializes in museum pieces,

antique clocks, real treasures. I've been to his shop. You must go with me once. It's fabulous. He's got . . ."

"Suddenly clocks bore me to death," Chris cut her off. "Let's get back to what's important. This idea of his is worth going after; I'll grant him that much."

"I have to find Mrs. Tummler."

"*You* don't. If Mrs. Tummler and her nephew are somehow mixed up in all this, they could be dangerous. One attack on your life is enough, at least it is for me. They haven't found the bastard yet either. He may still be around. Now promise not to play detective."

"I promise," said Lisa, but she had no intention of keeping her word.

17

Mrs. Tummler's nephew Heinrich was a good carpenter, but not reliable enough to be steadily employed. He preferred the bottle to a long day's work and had sponged on his aunt for years. He was also a stupid man. He had gone to pick up the luggage his aunt had left behind and been surprised to find the apartment guarded by a policeman who told him to wait in the foyer. But he had wandered into the study where, a few years ago, he had put up some shelves and cabinets for the Herr Professor. And there, on the floor, had lain something sparkling. At first he had thought it was a piece of glass catching a ray of sunlight, but then he had recognized it to be a good-sized diamond. When the policeman had come into the room to tell him he would have to wait outside, he had replied that he had just wanted to look at the shelves, maybe they needed some repair, the Herr Professor kept such heavy books on them; and while he was talking he had put his foot over the shining thing on the floor. Then he had pretended to tighten a shoelace and had picked it up. He still had it, and Mrs. Zeller's stolen jewelry, according to the papers, had been heavily insured. Each piece was described separately.

When he had got home with her luggage, he had found his aunt in hysterics over the Zeller murder and the apprehension of the professor, which she had just heard about over the radio. He had wondered why she had gone to pieces like that; she had never evidenced any special fondness for her employers. But there had been no calming her down. She had packed a knapsack, like a *wandervögel*—ridiculous at her age—and had taken off, saying she didn't know where she was going, nor did she have any idea when she would be back. Maybe never. But tonight or, rather, late in the afternoon she had turned up again. "Back," she had announced. She never wasted words. "And though I'm ready, you don't have to tell anyone I'm here." Ready for what? With her it could mean anything. She was a demon, that's what she was.

Then she told him.

"But how did you manage to get in?"

"On my feet. What's the matter with you?"

"The house is being watched. They're looking for you."

"Well, there was only one man, and he must have had a weak bladder. Anyway, I didn't have to wait long for him to leave." She disappeared into her room. An hour later the doorbell rang. He jumped.

The diamond had become the most important thing in his life. He hadn't been able to muster the courage yet to sell it. But was it safe in the tea canister now that his aunt was back? He'd have to think of another place to put it. He'd never done anything really illegal before. Being drunk or too hungover to go to work was no crime, but with the diamond in the house, he had the wild notion that any minute he'd be handcuffed and hauled off to jail.

The bell rang again, longer this time. "All right, all right," he muttered as he trotted back to the front door and peered through the peephole. A girl. Her voice was firm. "Open up," she said. "Police."

"Police?" He wasn't ready to believe her, but then, through the hole, he could see her flash a small disk. He had never encountered a policewoman. She looked frail, so he opened the door. Easy to strangle, he thought. But what good would that do him? "Let me see your identification."

The girl hesitated, and with that he knew it was a ruse. He tore it from her hand—a metal cap, the kind that was screwed on a gas tank. He pounced on her, his hands went around her throat. With all the breath she could muster, Lisa screamed. He hadn't dreamed a girl could scream with such volume.

A door opened behind him. His aunt, in a nightgown, bed jacket, her gray hair in a neat ponytail, tied with an elastic. "What's going on here?"

He loosened his hands and the girl said hoarsely, "I'm Lisa Tanner, and you're Hedwig Tummler."

"I thought you'd come to see me," said Mrs. Tummler. "Let her go, you idiot."

He couldn't help himself; he stuck out his leg and she fell over it. That much at least he got out of it. Mrs. Tummler helped Lisa up, then she slapped her nephew's face. "He's crazy," she said. "It's my fault. I raised him. Never raise other people's children," and to him, "get out! And don't listen at the door. I'm going to check."

She held out a hand to Lisa and led her along a short passage into a small, immaculate room. A cuckoo popped out of its door in a clock on the wall and sounded eleven times as she sat down. "He's a good boy though, in certain ways," she said. "He obeys me, and that's something to be thankful for. And he's kept all sorts of people away. Lies all the time. It comes easy to him. You look done in. Have an enzian. It'll warm your insides."

She took a bottle that was almost full from the knapsack, which she hadn't unpacked, and two small glasses from a cupboard. "Drink it. You need something to pep you up."

She stretched out on the bed. The linen smelled as if it had been dried on a sunny meadow. She crossed her well-shaped legs at the ankles. "For a long time," she said, "I didn't approve of you. A young woman taking up with a married man. I'm old-fashioned, and I'm not ashamed to admit it. I believe in matrimony. My husband . . . well, he died. Long ago. Still I revere his memory, never had a man after him. Stupid of me, perhaps." She shrugged. "But you can get over sex as you can get over anything, I mean, the need for it. At least I could. One shouldn't generalize, of course. And then I began to realize what kind of person she was. Even before you came into his life."

Lisa swallowed the enzian in one gulp. Miraculous that such a sharp drink could be extracted from the tiny blue gentian.

"Well, I learned to despise her. If she had at least tried

to make him happy, but not even that. Not that I'd have condoned her behavior, but it would have made it understandable."

She stuck the tip of her tongue into the small high-stemmed glass, took a nip and smiled. "I come from the mountains. Used to work at the Waldhaus. As a housekeeper. Then it got too much for me with all the foreigners demanding this and demanding that, and I saw her ad in the paper. Only two people to take care of. Good neighborhood. New house. I like new equipment. And I always could cook. Bless my mother. She began to teach me when I was eight. So I took the job. And liked it. They didn't work me hard, and he was always satisfied with everything I did. Used to pat me on the shoulder. 'Thank God for you.' Who wouldn't like to hear that? It seems she was hard to get along with. Well, rest her soul, although I must say she deserved it, the way she carried on."

"I didn't know you sympathized with him."

"Sympathized with him? He's a great man and a fine human being, and the two don't always go together." She took another nip, noticed that Lisa's glass was empty and pointed to the bottle. "Help yourself." Lisa did. "Oh, I know he is self-centered," Mrs. Tummler went on, "but so are most men as dedicated to their work as he is. But what I admire about him most is that he can't be bought. The way he sticks with Signor Martelli, when he could make so much money with some of the big firms that have approached him."

What a lot of information domestics pick up, Lisa thought. Just like nurses and hairdressers.

"Then why did you hide when everybody was looking for you?" she asked.

"Didn't want to be questioned before I'd figured things out. That's reasonable, isn't it?"

"It certainly is," said Lisa, "and will make your testimony all the more valuable."

"You can give me some more too." Mrs. Tummler held out her glass. "My testimony," she said, as Lisa filled it, "will be a bombshell. I know the name of the murderer."

"The name of the murderer?"

Mrs. Tummler downed her drink, shook herself, and

said, "Her last lover. The one she was really crazy about. Sometimes she called him Graham, but mostly Gram."

She reached under her pillow and drew out a piece of paper, once ripped up and crinkled, but now pieced together and stuck on cardboard. "Found it in her waste-paper basket. Worked on it all that night, I mean now after I left. A few pieces are missing, but they're small. It's still legible."

Lisa held out her hand, trying to keep it steady as her excitement rose. But Mrs. Tummler clutched the piece of cardboard to her chest. "I'll read it to you . . . 'Gram, my love, I can't do it. It would kill Anton to find his papers gone. But apart from that, it simply isn't in me. I've thought of your proposal, I want to marry you, I know we could be happy and good for each other, but the price is too high. Aren't you exaggerating when you say it's a matter of life or death? I can't believe they'd kill you if you don't get what they're after. But to think of you. . . .'" Mrs. Tummler looked up, "Here the hand-writing changes; the letters get bigger and all on a down-ward slant: 'But to think of life without you . . . I can't. It would kill me. Call me. I need time to think it over, so do you. And if it has to be, go away, where you feel safe. I'll come to you wherever you are. I love you, I need you, I can't live without you.'"

For quite some time Lisa was silent, then she said, "Do you know his last name?"

"Foley. Graham Foley."

"May I use your phone?"

"It's in the hall."

But before Lisa could finish dialing, there was a ring at the door, an exchange of loud voices. Lisa recognized Wieland's. "It didn't take them long to find me, did it?" said Mrs. Tummler.

Wieland came into the room. He stared at Lisa. "What are you doing here?"

"Never mind," said Lisa. "But Beaulieu was right. She has a letter that will prove it."

18

Zeller tried everything he could think of to drive the restlessness out of his body. Yoga. It didn't work. He simply couldn't make his mind go blank, nor could he organize his thoughts. They insisted on storming through his mind, returning always to the morning he had found Helene dead, and to Stadelmann saying, "There is no bail for a murder suspect."

He exercised vigorously. When he was taken out for fresh air, he never walked, he jogged. He read the papers; he read his medical journals from cover to cover; he tried to listen to the small radio fixed to the wall over his bed, with its carefully selected programs. Nothing registered. He played chess with himself, solved mathematical problems. He tried to find solace in the knowledge that other men had suffered worse fates, that at least he wasn't being tortured or made to suffer indignities, hunger, thirst. How had other men endured solitary confinement for years? Being chained, starved? He tried to think of those, unlike himself, who had never been able to do what they wanted, who were in a way imprisoned by life itself with a job they hated, who could no more break from the mundaneness of their existence than he could break out of prison. Outwardly he looked the picture of health, his muscle tone was better than before, but inwardly he was devouring himself, laden with an explosive charge that seemed ready to detonate just when he thought he had calmed down. A couple of times he had come close to attacking a guard. Only by telling himself over and over again, sometimes aloud, that any violence on his part would harm his case, did he manage to keep his hands in his pockets. And there were moments when he thought he was going mad. They were the worst.

"This came for you," said the guard, holding out a medical journal. He had asked for several new magazines a couple of days ago, and this was one of them. He began to leaf through it, scanning the titles. On one of the pages in the inner margin he noticed a small number had been penciled. Then he saw that many pages had been marked. He leafed back to start with the first: 19, 9, 13, 21, 12, 1, 20, 5 . . . at the end he had noted forty-one numbers. He stared at them. Five of them were followed by a slash, three others by a double slash. The numbers went no higher than 21. He was reminded of how they had cheated in school, spelling out letters numerically to form question or answer. Quickly he set to work, and to his ever-growing astonishment they added up to: "Simulate/pain/Appendix/Ask/for/doctor/after/dark."

The meaning was clear, but who was behind this? He had seen Stadelmann yesterday, but Stadelmann was the last person to do anything against the law. Lisa? Impossible. This sort of thing was beyond her capacities. Or was it? Actually he didn't care. All he could think of was that it might mean *out*.

He ripped out the pages, tore them into small pieces, and flushed them down the toilet. He refused to eat lunch with the excuse that he was feeling nauseated. He lay down on his bed and closed his eyes. Once in a while he moaned softly—in the afternoon, louder, and when the guard wanted to know what was wrong, he told the man that he had a pain in his side, showed him where. A great excitement filled him, and the sweat on his forehead was profuse.

Night fell. Zeller was writhing in pain. He told the guard, "I know it's my appendix, damn it."

The prison doctor came. Examined him. Zeller placed his pain in the proper area. "Should have had it out long ago, but could never give it the time."

The prison doctor thrust a thermometer into his mouth. "No temperature."

"If you want to wait until it ruptures, I can produce a temperature for you."

The doctor left, looking perplexed. Twenty minutes later Dr. Fehr from the Kantonspital came in. He confirmed Zeller's diagnosis. "And I don't think we should wait, don't you agree?"

A good half hour later the ambulance of the Kantonspital pulled up in the courtyard. Zeller was moved gently from his bed onto a collapsible rolling stretcher. Two guards accompanied him; one sat with the driver, the other with Zeller and Dr. Fehr. The heavy traffic had eased up; they reached emergency in no time. Two orderlies were waiting to take him inside the familiar building. One of them was a tall, lanky fellow with black shiny eyes and dark hair falling to his collar. As he pushed the stretcher toward the bedlift, with one of the police guards following, he told Zeller, "Professor Buerkli is going to operate." Once inside the elevator, he made no room for the other orderly or the policeman to enter, but pressed the button before either of them could get in. "Take the other one," he called out to them as the door closed.

The elevator ascended; Zeller could see the floor letters light up as they passed one after the other, passed surgery, and stopped on Floor F—the sixth floor. "Get up," said the young man. "Walk to the platform as fast as you can." He pushed Zeller forward with a gun in his hand, guiding him with it along the landing pad and into the waiting helicopter, its blades whirring. The aircraft rose, circled the roof, and took off in the direction of Basel.

19

"Why . . . why did he do it?" Stadelmann's voice was suddenly so loud, a secretary came in to ask if anything was wrong. He sent her out of the room and looked from Lisa to Wieland, from Wieland to Chris, from Chris to Beaulieu. Zeller's escape had made headlines and been reported over the air.

"I don't see why his escape should be proof he is guilty of the crime." Lisa spoke quietly. "It may have been a fool thing to do, but I told all of you, and you, Herr Doktor, know, that he could stand almost anything except the loss of his freedom. And to him things were beginning to look hopeless." If only she had been able to tell him about Mrs. Tummler's letter. "For him it was either a case of getting out or suicide. At least that was my impression when I saw him. He was desperate."

She meant what she said. The thought that Zeller had escaped because he was guilty was something that hadn't entered her mind. Surprise, disbelief, a feeling of having been abandoned, but not the thought that this proved he had murdered Helene.

"You fail to realize," said Stadelmann, "that his escape was no impulsive act. It was well planned, well organized. Others were involved." He sounded angry, and for the first time as though he could no longer believe his friend was innocent.

"The helicopter was found abandoned on a meadow near Basel," said Wieland. "It was registered under the name of Hugo Schmidt, a citizen of Argentina. Privately owned. The pilot, a Czech, duly cleared all formalities to fly to Zurich and land at the hospital." He took a sheaf of papers from his jacket pocket, leafed through them, found what he was looking for and said, "Emil Schultz. No trace of him so far. The police assumption that they made their way on foot from Basel into Germany proved to be correct. A private jet took off from Stuttgart this morning, again registered under the name of Hugo Schmidt. On board: Franz Willert, Mercurio Bongrani, Willy Suter—Suter is the pilot—Karl Sandhofer, copilot. One of the men was in a wheelchair. All gave their names as residents of Stuttgart. The Stuttgart police has reported that no persons thus named are registered as residing in the city of Stuttgart."

"What could make one weep," Beaulieu murmured, and looked as if he really could have broken into tears any moment, "is the irony of it all. Just when we had a practically foolproof angle for the defense, he chooses to commit this idiocy. Why should a man with a clear conscience and a good chance of being acquitted . . ."

"If Zeller has gone to Argentina, will they extradite him?" asked Lisa.

"South American countries," said Stadelmann, "have a strange way of handling their obligations to other countries. You may recall how long a certain Dr. Wiesenthal, who set himself up as an avenger of the Jewish massacre, pleaded to have some well-known Nazis extradited."

"Then I'm glad he did it," said Lisa. "Now he may have a chance to live free, at least until we've been able to prove his innocence."

"Well, Mrs. Tummler's evidence clearly indicates that, doesn't it?" said Beaulieu.

"What we have to do," said Chris, "is find Graham Foley."

"And so far," said Wieland, "we haven't had much luck. He checked out of the Savoy the day before the murder; he liquidated his safe-deposit box at the Schweizerkreditanstalt the day after. There is no trace of a Graham Foley having entered or left Switzerland, nor is anyone by that name registered in the country now. We presume he is traveling under an assumed name, with forged papers."

115

"But we've got to find him," said Lisa.

"Yes," said Wieland, "we've got to find him."

As they parted, both Chris and Beaulieu invited Lisa to have dinner with them, but she shook her head. She asked Wieland to stay for a moment, and after the others had left she said to him, "I would appreciate it if you would come up to my apartment around nine o'clock. Or if you want to make it earlier, I'd be happy to give you a bite to eat."

Inspector Wieland looked flustered. He was not in the habit of taking young women out or visiting them. Since his wife's death, he moved strictly in the circle of their old friends and acquaintances, who included him socially whenever he felt like joining them. Nor had he ever slept with any women except his wife, unless you wanted to count the times before he got married, and then he had used every precaution he could think of. He wasn't actually planning to marry again. If one of his old friends were to die, he might take his widow for a wife, someone he'd always known and could rely on, but faced with Chase's and Beaulieu's invitations to take Lisa out, he didn't want to seem less gallant. So, although the idea of dining with her embarrassed him, he rose to the occasion.

"I know a little restaurant," he said, almost stammering —her apartment was definitely out—"nothing much, but I'll be happy to pick you up around eight."

Lisa smiled. "I'll be downstairs." She gave him her address, which she realized he must know, but she wanted to avoid all professional aspects of their relationship, and he went through the gesture of jotting it down in a little black book in which there were very few addresses.

They went to a small place near the university where the food was cheap but good, and he ordered a Bernerplatte, sauerkraut piled high with Viennese sausage, a pork chop, broiled ham, and smoked sausage, enough to fill the hungriest man's stomach, while she asked for "Geschnetzeltes." They both drank beer. She ate almost as heartily as he did, she passed him the rolls, the salt, without being asked. There was something about the meal and the girl that made him feel at home.

In the course of his work he had encountered every

type of woman, rich and flighty, rich and proper, conventional and bohemian, all the way down to whores and madams, but he had never met socially with a woman who had quite openly been the mistress of a married man, and he suddenly began to understand what made this young nurse so attractive to such different types as Zeller, Chase, and Beaulieu. But still he couldn't imagine why she should have preferred his company to the elegant, amusing Beaulieu or the devoted consular officer who wanted to marry her. He felt uncomfortable about it until she told him quite frankly why she had wanted to see him privately. "Of course I want you to do me a favor, Herr Inspektor."

He was a man of few words, so he asked quite bluntly, "What?"

Lisa appreciated his directness. Altogether she found she could speak more easily to Wieland than to Stadelmann or Beaulieu, even to Chris. There was something about the inspector that was reassuringly down to earth. "I want you to come with me to Mrs. Tummler's apartment."

"I made an appointment with her for tomorrow."

"I know it's stupid of me, but when something's on my mind, I hate to put it off."

"And what is on your mind?"

"I have the feeling she may know more than she has told us so far. This man, Graham Foley, if he was after Zeller's findings, don't you think he might also have had something to do with Zeller's escape?"

"It is possible." The thought had of course crossed his mind.

"And don't you think it is also possible that Mrs. Tummler might be able to give us more information on him? Certainly she is the only person we know who could. Perhaps I could get it out of her, but I'm afraid to go there alone. I told you how her nephew attacked me when I went to see her. I don't necessarily want you to come in with me, but if you'd just hang around in case he attacks me again. Women talk better alone, anyway, differently, than in front of a third person, particularly an official. Besides, he may not let me in. Can you pick a lock?"

It made Wieland smile. "First thing I had to learn."

"Then let's go now," she said.

Wieland didn't like to have anyone interfere with what he had planned, and usually, he thought with pride, his timing was right, but he had also learned to respect other people's hunches, and this girl, so unshakable in her faith in Zeller's innocence . . . or did all women in love believe in their men? In any case, she appealed to him in her eagerness.

"It's late," he said, "but that's when people feel lonely and are ready to talk."

In Fluntern, where Mrs. Tummler lived, the streets were quiet and few of the windows showed light. They rang the bell to her apartment; nobody answered. After three rings, Wieland inserted a piece of plastic between the latch and the door jamb, and the door opened. There was no sound. Inside, everything was dark.

"I've got a flashlight," said Lisa. "I know where her room is. Along the passage, turn a corner, second door on the right."

"I think I'd better turn over my job to you." Lisa walked on ahead. She knocked on the door of Hedwig Tummler's bedroom. There was no answer. She called, but her voice was the only sound. Finally she opened the door. The room was dark, quiet, not even the sound of a sleeper's light breathing. "Mrs. Tummler?"

Lisa felt for the light switch, found it to the right of the door. The ceiling light went on, throwing a rosy glow over Mrs. Tummler in her bed.

"I'm sorry," said Lisa. "I know it's late and I guess we should have telephoned first, but it's urgent."

Mrs. Tummler gave no indication she had heard. Lisa walked over to the bed. She touched Mrs. Tummler's hand. It was cold, and when she let go it fell to her side. "Mrs. Tummler!" Lisa's voice was high-pitched with fear. Wieland came in. "Anything wrong?"

"I can't rouse her."

Wieland bent over the still body, felt her pulse, laid his hand on her chest. "She's dead."

"She must have died in her sleep," said Lisa. "That's the way I'd like to go. No pain. No apprehension."

Wieland, who had raised Mrs. Tummler's head, spoke quietly as it fell back. "She was murdered," he said, "by a strong blow to the nape of the neck. Look." He pointed to a small tangle of hair on the floor beside the bed. "He must have pulled her up by her hair. Where's the telephone? I've got to call homicide."

20

There were no stars the night Zeller was pushed out of the helicopter and made to walk across a meadow and into woodland, on a path that wound endlessly between trees and came out on a highway, where a car stood waiting. Every now and then he could feel the dark-haired man's gun at his back, hurrying him on.

"What's all this about?" he asked.

"You'll find out in due time."

"I'm being kidnapped."

"You may call it that."

"Who are you?"

"That's not important. Important is that you are Franz Willert, from Hamburg, an executive of Lufthansa. Your papers are in order, but you can't talk. You've had a stroke which has left you suffering from aphasia. There's a wheelchair in the trunk of the car. As soon as we get to the airport, we'll put you in it. And you stay in it until we've taken off. You're going to see a specialist in Paris. If you try to get away, I'll shoot. This gun has a silencer, so nobody will hear a sound, and if you fall down, it will be just another stroke."

"How do you intend to cross the border? They're very thorough."

"You passed the border before you got into this car," said the young man. "Now sit still while I dye your hair."

It was only then that Zeller noticed the curtains drawn across the windows, as in classic limousines. He was by no means as calm as he pretended to be, but realized there was nothing he could do.

"My name is Mercurio," said the young man. "Mercurio Bongrani."

By the way he pronounced the Italian pseudonym— and it had to be a pseudonym, Zeller thought—he was made aware of the fact that Mercurio had been speaking perfect English, with a slight Oxford accent. Now he produced a satchel from which he took a bottle, a brush, a comb, and a towel. He draped the towel around Zeller's shoulders, and while he was doing so, Zeller saw that the pilot of the helicopter, sitting in front with the driver, had turned in his seat and had a gun trained on him.

Mercurio wet the brush with some thick black liquid from the bottle and brushed it several times through Zeller's blond hair. "We should let it set for half an hour, until it really takes, then it should be rinsed off, but since we have no water and not enough time, we'll just have to do the best we can." About fifteen minutes later, he wet a handkerchief from another bottle and cleaned away the color where it had leaked over the hairline and onto the skin behind Zeller's ears and neck. Then he combed the dye through Zeller's hair, cleaned the skin again, and opened a small case. The case contained dark contact lenses. "Put them in yourself," he said. "They'll make your eyes smart a little and you'll have to blink a lot until you get used to them. You also may not see very well. Since you don't wear glasses, we couldn't get you prescription lenses. Try not to lose them. The damn things have a way of slipping out. Here are sun glasses. Wear them. And this hat. Keep it on, even if some passport official asks you to remove it. You're hard of hearing and you don't understand him. If it has to come off, I'll remove it for you, just in case some of the dye has come off on the lining. Your hair should be dry by now. Let me feel it."

He felt it and nodded.

"You must have been a makeup artist," said Zeller, whose sense of the ridiculous was getting the better of him.

"I've been many things," said Mercurio. "In our world you have to be able to do anything to make a living. The art of adaptation is requisite to survival."

So it is, thought Zeller. He hadn't been able to adapt to being locked up and had got himself into this fool situation without giving any serious thought as to who might be so interested in getting him out of jail. Now it seemed incredible that he should have thought only of Stadelmann and Lisa as possibly having had a hand in his escape. He also realized that in the eyes of most people, especially the law, he had escaped because he had expected to be found guilty. It had never occurred to him that he was being kidnapped; to him the whole crazy escapade had meant only one thing—freedom. But if he had known it beforehand, he would have done the same thing. If I'd waited three months longer for the trial to come up, he told himself, I would have gone mad. He understood then that loss of freedom corrupted you—gradually but certainly it forced you to act, to accept any chance to break free, no matter who offered that chance, and to what other ends. These people seemed to need him. Why?

Mercurio opened a suitcase and produced a pair of socks, a business suit, dark blue, pinstriped. "Put these on."

When he handed Zeller a pair of shoes, which surprisingly fitted, Zeller said, "I could have done with these on our trek through the woods. Bedroom slippers were hardly the thing for that."

The lights of a large city illuminated the sky, but that was all he could see through the contact lenses when they got out at an airport, because his eyes were watering. When the car stopped in front of the departure building, the driver opened the trunk of the car, unfolded a wheelchair, and Mercurio and the pilot helped Zeller into it with great solicitude. A few seconds later an elderly man appeared, bowed, introduced himself as Otto Koblenz. "I am delegated to see that you won't encounter any delays."

A Hansa official. My God, thought Zeller, the whole thing has been arranged with such care. . . . "If you would be good enough to let me have your passports," the man was addressing Mercurio, who handed them to him. "You can take Herr Willert to our private waiting room. Do have a drink and relax until I call you."

They had barely taken the first sip when Koblenz came back, stamped passports in hand. "Your jet is ready to take off, but if you want to finish your drinks, I'll see what I can do about delaying it."

"No need for that," said Mercurio. "I'm sure we'll find anything we may want on it, am I right?"

"Of course. Everything has been taken care of," said Koblenz.

And everything had been taken care of, down to the last detail. Zeller, in his wheelchair, was rolled into a van that drove him and his companions to where the jet stood waiting on the tarmac at the far end of the airfield. The noise of the big engines was too loud to hear Koblenz's polite wishes for a good flight. The steps were pulled in, the door closed, and approximately three minutes later the plane took off. Pilot and copilot disappeared into the cockpit, Mercurio into the galley. Zeller could see three comfortable beds which looked inviting enough to lie down on right away. The long walk through the woods had tired him, but he was too excited, and—idiotic as it might seem—too amused to think of sleep.

Mercurio reappeared, doubling now as steward. "Toilet along the passage, to the right. What about some caviar and vodka? I think all of us could do with some food."

"Privately hired jet, I presume?"

"Privately owned."

"By whom?"

Instead of answering, Mercurio spooned a generous portion of caviar onto Zeller's plate, poured him a large glass of well-iced vodka, and brought two other trays, with equally large helpings, to the pilots. The caviar made Zeller think of Russia. Was that where they were heading? He had never been to the Soviet Union and would have had nothing against being taken there now. It didn't occur to him in his moment of euphoria that, having been forcefully freed from prison, he might also be kept by force in whatever country they were taking him to.

"Where are we going?" he asked, when Mercurio took the seat next to him.

Mercurio gave him the same answer as before. "You'll find out. Don't waste your time and mine asking questions I won't answer. There are cold cuts, salad, different kinds of cheese, and if you want coffee, I'll make you an espresso. Would you care for some wine with the rest of the meal?"

Zeller ate ravenously, as if the prison food had never been enough to satisfy him. He had never tasted tenderer roast beef, and it was rare; the pickles were not too salty, and the round of Brie just at the runny stage. The espresso was strong, without being bitter, the brandy over fifty years old and as smooth as heavy cream. He enjoyed it all, every bite and sip. Whoever his host was, he knew how to feed his guests.

After a while he went to the washroom. Mercurio knocked and came in with his makeup bottles. "Now let me do a good job."

Somehow Zeller had neglected to look at himself in the mirror, only removed the lenses which, as he had been warned, were irritating. Now, when Mercurio turned Zeller's head so that he could face the mirror, he could hardly believe it was the same man who had been prodded with a gun to a waiting helicopter on the roof of the Kantonspital. How easy it was to disguise oneself. Just to see what the dark lenses did for him, he put them back in and for a moment couldn't get over how much their blackness changed his face. Transformation from Saxon to Latin.

Mercurio provided a pair of fresh pajamas. They too fitted. Zeller began to hum. It was all too fantastic to be real. A boy's dream of adventure. In the cabin he threw himself on one of the beds. The covers had been folded back. A glass of milk stood on a table beside it. "Drink it," said Mercurio. "The caviar was rather salty. But if you'd prefer scotch . . ."

Zeller drank the milk. It was ice cold and sweet, just the way he liked it. "There's a good Bergman film on board," said Mercurio, "also a choice of others if you prefer something lighter."

"Right now I prefer not to be disturbed by anything that makes noise," said Zeller.

"Very well." Mercurio went off to sit with the pilots and listen to the radio. Zeller lay back. He loved flying. The whole idea that man had conquered the sky had fascinated him ever since his father had read the story of

Icarus to him. He pushed aside the curtain across the window nearest to him. They were traveling with the night, west therefore. Clouds were chasing each other between stars that blinked with dazzling brightness. He looked out for a long time. Finally he fell asleep.

He was awakened a few hours later, or perhaps they had been flying longer than that. It took a while to shake off a strange drowsiness. He felt groggy, and there was no doubt in his mind that Mercurio had slipped something into his drink.

"Put your lenses back in," said Mercurio. "We're landing in a while for refueling. If an official comes on board, don't speak. Pretend to be asleep." There was a gun in his hand again. He just let it be seen without wasting a word of explanation.

A perfect landing. A man in uniform. Zeller wished countries would be more imaginative in designing their uniforms. Suddenly he was furious that he couldn't tell where he was. Then the plane took off again and he was served breakfast—fresh fruit, coffee, hot cereal, scrambled eggs on the wet side. Whoever had kidnapped him knew his taste.

Hours of flight during which Mercurio put on two movies, without asking Zeller if it would disturb him or not. He had quite evidently lost his good humor, and Zeller wondered why. Had something gone wrong? He moved the curtain that covered a window, and Mercurio said sharply, "Don't do that." But Zeller had had a moment to see a rough sea beneath them in the graying light of dawn. He was told to dress. He did. Mercurio pulled a wide black scarf from his pocket. "What are you going to do with that?"

"What do you think?" Mercurio said rudely, and blindfolded him. So he was not to know where he was.

A twenty-minute wait. Zeller could tell by the faint shudder of the plane and a sinking feeling that the plane was descending. Blindfolded, all sensations were intensified. The noise of a door opening and he was led like a blind man down steps, across cement, and helped into a car. No wheelchair this time. The car took off, its siren screaming.

Zeller tried to push the black silk away from his eyes,

but a vicious slap on the hand made him stop. "I told you not to do that," said Mercurio.

"You almost broke my hand."

"And I'll break every bone in your body if you don't obey orders."

C'est le ton qui fait la musique, thought Zeller, and the tone had definitely changed.

He began to count to himself, in an effort to figure out how long they were driving; he tried to keep track of how many turns they took to right and left, how long they went straight, to gauge their speed. But perhaps, unseeing, motion too was accelerated in the mind. At last they stopped. Mercurio took his right arm and somebody else his left. He could feel the ground under his feet, not cement—dirt, a hard-trodden dirt road. Then there was a door—he was warned that the threshold was raised. A narrow passage—he could tell by the way the second man held his arm slightly backward; another door and then, without warning, the blindfold was removed. "And you can take the lenses out too," said Mercurio.

The room Zeller found himself in was large, almost like an artist's studio, and there were no windows in the walls, only a skylight in the ceiling. The glass was too high to show anything but sky, and unreachable.

"Welcome, Herr Professor," said a voice that sounded familiar. Before him stood a man on crutches, a man whose face seemed made of putty. Schmidt.

"What in the world are you doing here?"

"When I came to you some time ago and asked you to do me a favor, you turned me down."

"And I told you why," said Zeller, walking rapidly through the room to exercise his legs, stiff after the long flight. "I explained it all to you at the time. Ordinarily, as you rightly assumed, I would have been glad to find another human being ready to take the risk of an insufficiently tested vaccine, but you mentioned that the man in question was an important person, so I had to refuse. Even now I'm still trying it out only on convict volunteers."

"I saw you again, at your office, and you were very short, I'd say almost rude."

"I remember," said Zeller, and stopped pacing the
126

room as he recalled that day. "And I explained to you that just three days before, a man I had been treating had died. Right then I was in no mood to try it on anybody else."

Schmidt lit a cigarette. It looked like something a child had stuck into the mouth of a poorly built snowman. "I told you my friend was willing to take the risk."

"He's still alive?"

"He is. Why do you think we brought you here? But his condition has become more serious." He paused, crushed his cigarette, and continued. "Since you weren't willing to come of your own free will, and we were unable to secure your findings, we saw no other way but to bring you here by force."

"Here?" said Zeller. "Where am I?"

"For what you are going to do for us, you don't have to know," said Schmidt, "nor am I going to worry you further by telling you who your patient is. You already know that he is an important man . . . I made the mistake of telling you that, and all I am willing to add is that he is the closest friend and adviser of our head of government. To lose him would be tragic for this country. You are our last hope."

"And if I refuse."

"You will be sent back to Switzerland, or shot. That's not for me to decide."

"I see."

"I hope you do. You will have all the assistance you need and anything you ask for." He pointed to a table, bare except for a green folder. "Your patient's medical history. Read it when you have rested. His personal doctor will be glad to fill you in on anything that may be missing. I'll be in touch with you through Mercurio. He will be sleeping in the next room." He gestured to the left. "All you have to do is knock on the wall and he'll be at your disposal. Goodbye, Herr Professor, or *Gruetzi,* as they say in your country. And remember—we didn't go to all the trouble of getting you out of jail and flying you here if we didn't expect you to accommodate us."

He limped toward the door, knocked three times, walked out when the door opened, after which it fell shut again. Zeller could hear the crutches coming down hard on the floor of the passage, then their sound dying away. He went to the door. There was no handle. He went back to the bed, which stood alongside the wall on the other side of which Mercurio slept, and sank down on it.

He was not free. He had simply moved from one prison to another. At least in Switzerland he had known where he was; in this strange country, which everyone refused to call by name, he could only guess—by the long hours of flight through the night—that he was in the Western Hemisphere, probably Latin America. Brazil? Argentina? Chile? He wasn't even sure that he would be able to make himself understood by the people with whom he would be dealing. There would be no Stadelmann, no Lisa every week, if only for fifteen minutes. Nobody he could trust. And in the meantime, the situation in Zurich would remain, with escape added to the charges against him. As detail after detail penetrated his mind, he couldn't imagine what had possessed him to look upon this escape as a bizarre adventure. And where would it end? Where could it end? The treatment required three months to show any signs of improvement. Meanwhile, he could contact no one and no one could get in touch with him. The handleless door, if nothing else, told him that. He could have screamed with fury, frustration, desperation; instead he gave in to hysterical laughter. The ludicrousness of it all! This man on crutches, this caricature of a human being whom he had restored to life, suddenly the *deus ex machina* of his imprisonment.

Zeller got up, began to pace the room again, twenty-five steps from one wall to the other, thirty-two the other way. There was a bar at one end. He opened its cabinet, inspected the array of bottles, closed it again. Right now he couldn't afford to cloud his mind with liquor. On an iron stand stood a large round bottle. Distilled water. Perhaps the water in this country wasn't safe to drink. He hoped it was Argentina because he could speak a little Spanish. Not Brazil. He didn't speak Portuguese. He went over to the table and picked up the green folder, then put it down again without opening it. Now now. Not yet.

Why, for God's sake, hadn't he stuck with his surgical practice? What had caused him to take on one of the world's foremost killers? What made men try the impossible? Because, he told himself, some people would recognize nothing as impossible. Men risked their lives to conquer a great mountain. Because it was there. Others sailed the oceans in small boats, on rafts. Because of the challenge. Men went to the moon. Why? Why not? And this disease, opening up before him every day of his life, had challenged him. To heal, to prevent—these drives were inborn. He came from a line of doctors. His father, his grandfather; his great-grandfather, an imaginative quack had started it all. They had brought their commitment a long way. And with him, blessed with the best education of his time, had come creativity. You had a dream, it became an obsession, and when the dream showed a chance of being translated into reality, you became practical again. And practically speaking, what had happened to him was disaster piled upon disaster. Dream and fulfillment were to be snuffed out here, in the depths of a sinister maze.

The door opened almost noiselessly while Zeller was sitting on the floor engaged in yoga exercises. "What are you doing?" asked Mercurio.

"Shh," said Zeller. "Don't disturb me. Come back in twenty minutes." He went on, moving according to the rules, ignoring Mercurio, who left as silently as he had come and returned half an hour later. He seemed to expect praise for the extra ten minutes he had granted his prisoner. Still, Zeller said nothing.

"Have you looked at the folder?"

Zeller shook his head.

"Why not?"

Zeller shrugged.

"You'd better talk to me. Silence will get you nowhere."

"Haven't I already arrived at nowhere?"

"Why didn't you look at the folder?"

No answer.

"It is urgent to know your opinion. His doctor is waiting for it."

Zeller walked over to the bed and threw himself down on it.

"Don't be a fool. It won't help you. Unless you want to depart this life right now, cooperate. These people aren't patient."

Zeller didn't doubt that. "I am tired," he said. "I am stunned by what has happened. I'll look at the folder when I feel more rested and my mind is clearer. You can pass that on to your employer."

"What about some food?"

"I don't want anything right now. I'd like to be left alone."

"Very well. Later then. In the meantime, is there anything I can do for you?"

"Yes. I'd like a radio and a television set."

"That's out."

Zeller had expected this. "Then music," he said. "Round up a record player and some records. Classical music. Beethoven. Brahms. Haydn. Some rock and roll."

"I'll see what I can do. And when will you be ready to see our Dr. Grimstone?"

"When I've slept."

"You don't seem to give a damn whether you survive this little adventure or not."

"I don't give a damn."

It was the truth. At the moment he didn't care anymore what might happen to him.

"I wish I could feel like that," said Mercurio, "but I can't. You see, you've lived the best part of your life. I don't mean by that you're an old man, but you're over forty, and I'm not thirty yet. And there are things I want to do. Don't you see, we're in the same boat? If you don't cooperate, I'm dead too."

"Do you have the gall to stand there and appeal to me to save *your* skin?"

Mercurio's grin was disarming. For the first time Zeller saw the young man as physically handsome, even attractive, certainly to women. "I am appealing to your role as a saver of lives," said Mercurio, and left with a flourish.

21

The medical history of his unknown patient was frightening. AS had progressed to such an extent in the coronary arteries, Zeller doubted that his vaccine could be effective. The cinearteriogram revealed almost complete occlusion of both the main right and left arteries. The result of the blood test showed a cholesterol level of over 500 mg%. The lipoproteins were exceedingly high.

"It's a miracle he isn't dead," Zeller said to the English doctor, William Grimstone, who had entered his room a short while before. Impossible to know if this was his real name, but he certainly looked like a typical Englishman, if there was something that could be called typical in any race. He was immaculately dressed in white linen slacks and blue blazer, his shirt was open at the neck, but his throat, from which it would have been easier to tell his age, was hidden by a dark blue ascot. His manners, too, were of a British gentility Zeller had always admired and sometimes tried to imitate, without much success—easy, polite, self-assured, and above all, serene—and all this without a trace of arrogance. A man in his late forties or early fifties, Zeller guessed. The ruddy complexion of the rather narrow face spoke of outdoor activity; his red hair was a surprise, receding at the hairline and showing a few thin spots at the back of the head. He also had a short, well-groomed beard, which he fingered when he spoke. The glance of his blue eyes was clever, alert, and penetrating, rather like that of a racoon peering out from a hollow tree. Zeller couldn't help wondering how this Englishman had come to be the private physician of "a very important person" in a foreign government. Perhaps a ship's doctor? They often chose not to return to their native land, either because they couldn't make a distinguished enough career there or because they became entranced with one of their many ports of call. He would have liked to ask, but felt sure that whatever the answer, it would not be the truth. And quite possibly Dr. Grimstone wasn't a medical man at all.

"He's had two strokes, the last one major. It affected his left side and his speech, but that has improved. Therapy seems to be helping in so far as the paralysis is concerned. We have done our best, but it's not good enough. We are depending on your vaccine to restore him."

"I shall need freshly slaughtered calves," said Zeller. "Healthy animals. That is essential. Cultures will have to be made, and I want to check them. And everything has to be obtained under absolutely sterile conditions. I'd like to do what I have to do at the slaughterhouse, personally."

"I can get you whatever you want, under any conditions you prescribe."

"I'd rather go myself."

"But in case that isn't possible?"

"Make it possible," said Zeller.

For the first time it occurred to him that, even with the folder before him, the patient might be just a front to get hold of his vaccine. Schmidt didn't impress him as a man anxious simply to save a friend's life, nor did he give the impression of being such a great patriot, acting for the good of his country. What country? Zeller even doubted that it was Schmidt's. He had the feeling that they intended to watch his every move, but if it was their intention to pirate his work, he would make it difficult for them. And there was another reason why he wanted to go to the slaughterhouse himself—the possibility of finding out where he was, of contacting someone, anyone, who could help him.

"I need a freshly slaughtered calf every three days," he said. "In every case a blood culture must be made so that we may be absolutely certain the animal is healthy. I need a lab. If you'll let me have some paper, I'll make a list of the equipment I need."

He wrote down more than he actually required, having decided to throw in a number of false leads. And he would make the vaccine fresh every time; he would leave nothing refrigerated for them to examine.

"By the way," he said to Grimstone, as he handed the doctor his list, "what is your specialty?"

"Internal medicine."

"It may be necessary for me to have some help in the slaughterhouse, and later in the lab."

"I'll be glad to assist you."

"That would be a waste of your time. A nurse will do."

"I'll see what can be arranged."

Dr. Grimstone knocked on the wall, signaling that he wanted to leave. Zeller detained him. "Do you play chess?"

"Sorry."

"What about cards?"

"Never could work up any interest in them."

The door opened and Dr. Grimstone left. Zeller went back to his bed and fell on it. For the first time since he had been a child, he felt like crying.

22

Inspector Wieland lived in an apartment which was too large and too expensive, but he had never been able to bring himself to the point of moving out. He didn't look or behave like a sentimental man, yet he was. As long as he stayed in the apartment, he had the feeling that somehow his dead wife was still around and would stick her head in the door any moment to call him to dinner, or to ask him if he wanted anything, or to scold him for working so late. He kept all the rooms unchanged from when she was still alive, even to the flowers she favored—violets in the spring, zinnias during the summer, and chrysanthemums in autumn, and the window boxes were a show of geraniums and petunias, as they always had been. At Advent he would hang a wreath on the entrance door, and for Christmas he decorated a tree with the ornaments she had kept stored tidily in a box in the attic. He polished red apples, gilded a few walnuts, and bought chocolate rings and marzipan fruit to hang on the branches. The neighborhood children came in, as they always had done, to strip the tree before it was thrown out, leaving the shells of nuts scattered on the floor. Since housekeepers and cleaning women were not only a nuisance but asked too much for the few hours they worked, he kept the place himself. This didn't bother him. On the contrary, it permitted him to mull over the day's events while he put things where they belonged. A case of ordering mind and house at the same time.

134

It was two nights after Mrs. Tummler had been discovered dead. He had spent the intervening days trying to find a clue to who might have murdered her. With absolutely no success. Nothing tired him as much as failure. He didn't feel like doing anything, not even undoing his neatly made bed. When he was ready for a few hours sleep he'd doze off on the couch in the room his wife had jokingly called his "office," because it was furnished so sparsely—just a desk, a swivel chair, a couch, two chairs, and shelves filled with law books, forensic literature, and some well-preserved fairy tales which his grandmother had read to him as a child. Her picture, that of his wife, and another of his son, who had fallen to his death climbing the north wall of the Matterhorn, stood on his desk. He put them into a drawer which he kept empty for the purpose, because it distracted him to look at their beloved faces when he was trying to concentrate on the intricate aspects of a case.

Some of his friends had given him a new jigsaw puzzle for his birthday. He hadn't tried it yet. He opened the box and shook the cutouts carefully onto the shiny surface of the desk. Then he reached into his hip pocket and fished out a small piece of tissue paper which he unfolded, and dropped what was inside it in front of him on top of the box. It was a piece of red thread. He had found it and another like it under Mrs. Tummler's fingernails, just before Inspector Graubart had arrived. The police lab was working on the other one.

Wieland stared at the red thread, not for the first time. He had held it up against the reddish pink lampshade on Mrs. Tummler's bedside table. It hadn't matched. He had looked through the clothes in her closet. A red raincoat, a red skirt, a red embroidered dress. Odd how some elderly women suddenly took to bright colors. But neither coat, skirt, nor dress had been exactly the color he was looking for.

To all appearances there had been almost no struggle, and the rooms hadn't been touched. In the midst of his investigation, Mrs. Tummler's nephew had come home from an evening out, reeking of beer and fairly drunk, but he had sobered up fast when he had found himself surrounded by policemen. He had been questioned extensive-

135

ly, but the shocking news of his aunt's death seemed to have affected his mind, not normally sound. He didn't make sense, but protested over and over again that he was innocent, that he hadn't even come home for dinner that evening, that he had an alibi—three friends with whom he had gone out after work—an alibi that had proved valid. He couldn't seem to get it into his thick head that nobody was accusing him of murder. Any questioning as to his aunt's friends and acquaintances would have to wait.

The box from which Wieland had taken the puzzle was white. On it the red thread looked like a thin line of blood. Wieland couldn't concentrate on his puzzle. There was a lot of blue and gray in it, a seascape perhaps, or a mountain scene. A corner piece seemed to be missing. He began to look for it. It annoyed him that he couldn't find it. Finally it turned up in the cuff of his trousers. He breathed a sigh of relief. He took the photos of his dear ones out of the drawer, and suddenly he knew it! He knew where the red thread came from. They had been in Zermatt . . . how many years ago? Happiness always seemed so far away. They had been looking at the Matterhorn through a telescope when a man behind them had complained that they were taking too long. Wieland's son had relinquished his place. "What a pity there are no men climbing it," he had said. "I would like to have watched them. One day I shall try the north wall. Papa, what was the funny thing the impatient man was wearing in his buttonhole?"

At first Wieland hadn't known what the boy meant, and had asked for a description. "A narrow red ribbon."

"Ah, you mean the Legion of Honor," and Wieland had explained the decoration, instituted by Napoleon, as a military and civil order of merit.

The Legion of Honor. But he couldn't remember having recently seen anyone wearing it.

He got up and went into his bedroom. He'd sleep in his bed after all. He began to fold back the spread, the covers, arranged the pillows—he liked to sleep high—when it came to him. Stadelmann's office. Stadelmann, Chase, Lisa, and—Gustave Beaulieu. Gustave Beaulieu had worn the red Legion of Honor ribbon that afternoon.

23

Wieland couldn't sleep. He thought of calling Graubart, to report his suspicion, then told himself it was too early for that. A red thread wasn't much to go on. And a hunch. Hunches required corroboration. Mrs. Tummler might have been doing some embroidery that evening; a friend might have visited her wearing something red—a scarf, crocheted gloves . . . but it had been a murder all right, just like Helene Zeller's, with no attempt to make it look like suicide.

Something else occurred to him. If the murder of Zeller's wife was connected with the effort to steal Zeller's findings—and certainly the Graham Foley letter pointed to that—then Mrs. Tummler's death could be similarly connected. If Beaulieu was in any way involved, then perhaps it was in collaboration with this Foley, of whom there was still no trace. Beaulieu, however, was very much in evidence. Could he possibly have had the gall . . . it was Beaulieu who had brought up this whole idea of Zeller's findings *before* Mrs. Tummler had produced the Foley letter. But then, according to the old adage, the murderer returned to the scene of the crime, and a man could very well come forward with a theory that spelled out something he had just perpetrated.

On the following day—he thought it would never dawn—he called Graubart. "There are a few things on my mind. What about the lab report?"

"Not in yet."

"I see. Then, in the Zeller apartment inventory, wasn't there a clock missing? A quite valuable one?"

"Yes."

"Was there any description?"

"I think so. I'll look it up. Want me to call you back?"

"No. I'll wait."

He waited. A few minutes later Graubart was back on the wire. "A Louis XV ormolu cartel clock . . ."

"Hold it. Slower. I can't write that fast."

"A Louis XV ormolu clock. Du Tertre." Graubart spelled the name. "Value approximately twenty-four thousand francs."

"And no trace of it."

"No trace of anything to date."

"All right. Second: name and phone number of the landlord of the building Lisa Tanner lives in."

Another five minutes and he had it, another ten and he had the name and address of the former owner of the apartment Beaulieu had moved into a few days before the attack on Lisa. Hans Bruno. Living now in the district of Enge, working as an insurance agent of the firm Mayer Bros. and Co.

At nine-thirty he was ushered into Mr. Bruno's small, cagelike office. Mr. Bruno was horrified when Wieland identified himself. He insisted on calling his lawyer before answering any questions.

"By all means," Wieland told him, "but I think you could save yourself a fee because my questions are few and quite simple, and you don't have to answer them if you don't want to. For instance—you used to live in the Winterthurerstrasse, in a one-and-a-half-room apartment."

"Five years."

"Small, decent apartments in that neighborhood aren't easy to find. What made you move out?"

Mr. Bruno hesitated. He reached for the phone.

"If you want me to leave the room . . ."

"I'd appreciate it."

Wieland waited a few minutes in a narrow passage that smelled of tomcat. He lighted one of his *Stumpen*. As he was stepping on the match, Mr. Bruno came out and waved him back in. Pushing a chair forward, he said, "It's all right to tell you what happened. It was like this. One

138

day a man came here and wanted some insurance. For his clocks. Valuable ones. Not his own. He repaired and restored them. Of course he was already carrying insurance, but he didn't feel it was enough. He invited me out for a glass of beer, and in the course of the conversation he told me he was looking for a small apartment in the Winterthurerstrasse, and when I said that was where I lived, he seemed surprised. He said what I had was just what he wanted, one-and-a-half rooms in that particular neighborhood. I thought he wanted it for a girl friend, something like that, but of course I didn't ask. That was none of my business. First I said no, but then he offered me such a large sum of money to move out, I couldn't resist. It meant a little nest egg, if you know what I mean."

"I know what you mean," said Wieland, sizing up Mr. Bruno as an elderly bachelor with little chance of ever bettering his position with a bigger firm.

"I talked to my lawyer about it, and he said it was perfectly all right. I had a sublease contract, and the sum being offered me was none of the landlord's business."

"His name was Gustave Beaulieu?"

"How did you know?"

"I went there looking for you because I need some insurance, and I found his name on the plate over the bell."

"I'll be happy to have you as a client," said Mr. Bruno, and Wieland said he'd be back the following week with the necessary information. Then he asked Mr. Bruno if he could see Gustave Beaulieu's policy. "But that's confidential," protested Mr. Bruno.

"I realize that," said Wieland. "If I must, I'll go to headquarters and get a subpoena. You see, we're conducting an investigation on Gustave Beaulieu, nothing serious so far, but I have to see his policy."

That did it.

The list of clocks was astonishingly long, their value impressive, and near the bottom of the list, brought in for repair in July, a Louis XV ormolu clock. Du Tertre. Value approximately 24,000 francs. Belonging to Helene R. Zeller.

24

At ten-thirty sharp, Wieland was at Beaulieu's shop, a small store located off an alley leading to the Hotel Storchen. He tried the handle several times, then saw a small sign on the wall to the right. "Open between eleven and twelve and from five to six." Apparently Gustave Beaulieu didn't work very hard at his profession.

Wieland crossed the street and bought some seed packets at Samen Mauser's famous store. Then he went for a walk. He paused before crossing the Rathaus Bridge to take his first good look at *Vertical Structure 1973:* brilliantly enameled undulating bands rising out of a concrete base, high over his head in brash lilac, salmon pink, and a poisonous sulphuric green. He peered down at the small brass plaque: Gillian Louise White was the artist. Well . . . where cultural sophistication was concerned, he was modest; he didn't have the courage to agree that it was "junk," the opinion someone had scrawled across its base, but he could not get used to modern outdoor sculpture in steel, plastic, and bright acrylic. He never would. For that he was too old. Incongruous—to him—against the traditional medieval buildings. This one cut offensively into the scene, in his opinion.

He turned his back on it and faced the Limmat. As he walked on he scarcely noticed the sudden fog blanketing the mountains. Under the clouds, the water of Lake Zurich looked pale, like a silver plate that had been handled too often. A drizzle began, but stopped as unexpectedly as it had begun. Scraps of fog still lingered over the valleys, making it seem as if a first snowfall had invaded them, and the dissolving clouds, piled high behind the mountains, gave an illusion of the greater peaks beyond.

At five minutes past eleven he was back at the shop. It was still locked, but when he rang the bell it was answered by an attractive young Japanese girl in Western dress. "Please have a seat," she said, in perfect German, and Wieland sat down in a small room that was carpeted wall to wall in gray. There were two French chairs, apparently genuine, and a small Louis XV writing desk with a telephone on it. A few seconds later Beaulieu appeared, as always dressed immaculately, but there was no Legion of Honor ribbon in his lapel.

"Sorry to keep you waiting, Monsieur Wieland. I was working. But of course I am happy to see you. Our mutual concerns keep you very much on my mind. What can I do for you?"

"Something different this time," said Wieland. "You see, I inherited a clock, a quite nice piece, I think also quite valuable. French. It's set between two Kendler swans and mounted on bronze. It's suddenly stopped."

"I can probably fix it for you. Do you have it with you?"

"No. But I'll bring it around, if you'd be good enough to look at it." He grinned. "A not too expensive look."

Gustave Beaulieu smiled. "Come into my workshop," he said, pushing open the door through which he had entered.

Wieland found himself in a large room, with clocks covering almost all the wall space. Near the window stood a work table, artificial lighting over it, instruments neatly spread out on it, wheels, large and small, pendulums, springs, all the paraphernalia of clock repair. "If you're interested in clocks, I have a book here on their history." Beaulieu picked it up. "I'll be glad to lend it to you. You know, they weren't made in Europe until the thirteenth century, but Pope Sylvester II is given credit for having invented them as far back as A.D. 996. Of course I've been fascinated by clocks as far back as I can remember."

"But you have a fortune here," said Wieland.

"Unfortunately not mine." Beaulieu pushed forward a

chair for Wieland to sit on. "They belong to my customers. That's how I meet so many interesting people, people rich enough to afford art as a hobby. And art to them means antiques, especially today, with monetary values in chaos. They have inherited these clocks or bought them at auction, as an investment. Most have been neglected and are in need of repair. A clock needs care, like a plant. I worked once, with others, on the clock on the Munich town hall, the one with the revolving figures that spring into action at noon. I am sure you know it. Ah yes, I've repaired quite a few famous ones and am considered an authority in my field, which isn't meant to sound like bragging. After all, I've devoted myself to nothing else all my life."

"Oh, before I forget," said Wieland, "I had to go through the inventory of the Zeller apartment the other day. A rather valuable clock is missing. It's been put on the list of stolen articles. Suddenly it occurred to me . . . the thieves might have tried to sell it, and if so, your shop would have been a likely place to try."

"What kind of a clock was it?"

"I've written it down," said Wieland, fumbling in his pocket for the paper. "Here it is. A Louis XV ormolu clock. Du Tertre."

Beaulieu smiled. "Anyone coming to me with a Du Tertre clock to sell would have a buyer, easily. But I'd be extra careful to find out where he got it."

"It's valued at about twenty-four thousand francs."

"And so it should be. Have you ever seen a Du Tertre clock? I have one here." He pointed to a clock on the wall, ornately set in a gilt frame, carved flowers, acanthus leaves.

"When did that come in?"

"I'll have to look." Beaulieu read what was on the tag attached to the clock. "My assistant signed for it, but he's not here. I'll have to check in the ledger."

He called for the Japanese girl and asked her to bring in the ledger. He found nothing in January, February, but in July there was an entry: A Louis XV ormolu clock. Du Tertre. For repair. Helene R. Zeller. And the address.

"You're making a mistake. It wasn't stolen, but delivered here for repair."

142

"What a strange coincidence," said Wieland, "it must have been just a few days before her murder."

"Strange indeed."

"Why hasn't it been repaired?" Wieland asked.

Gustave Beaulieu shook his head, smiling. "Ah, Monsieur Wieland, the repair of a valuable clock can be time-consuming. One has to resign oneself to anywhere from three to six months, longer if the parts to be replaced are hard to find. Which may be the case with the Zeller clock. I don't know. The question is, what do I do with it now?"

"That's not for me to decide," said Wieland. "I'll find out and let you know. Have you any idea who brought it in? Maybe Mrs. Tummler?"

"That I can't say," said Beaulieu. "It may have been brought in, or my delivery boy could have picked it up. Puri may be able to help you out on that."

"And who is Puri?"

"My assistant. You see, I'm not always here, in fact I have to travel quite a bit. And I can leave Puri in charge. He's good, one of the best."

"And when will he be back?"

"Next week, I sincerely hope."

"Will you let me know as soon as he gets back?"

"Certainly," said Beaulieu. "I'm very glad we found the clock here."

"So am I," said Wieland. "Thank you."

25

Without much hope, but impelled by something like the instinct of a hunting dog, Wieland drove to the Tummler apartment. The nephew opened up after he had rung the bell several times. "What's wrong now?" He was wiping the sleep from his eyes. "Doesn't a fellow have a little rest coming to him . . . after all I've been through . . ." He went back to his room and slammed the door, apparently totally disinterested in what the police might be after this time.

Wieland made no effort to detain him. He went straight to the kitchen, which he remembered as being neat and clean. It was a mess. Dirty dishes everywhere, cabinet doors open, the garbage can full to overflowing. Spreading two towels on the floor, he shook out the contents. Empty beer cans, two empty bottles of cheap wine, stale bread, crushed wrappers. Nothing for him. He opened the door to the small living room. A dining table, four chairs, the dust gathering on everything. A sofa, freshly upholstered, two armchairs with antimacassars, the cushions crushed. He stuck his hands into all cracks in chairs and sofa and came up with some crumpled tissue, a pencil with no point, a ten-rappen coin, some nutshells. He went to the bathroom, and there was the nephew, relieving himself.

"Can't you knock?"

"Couldn't you have locked the door?"

"I'm not used to people snooping around." But his hands were shaking.

All he wanted was for Wieland to get out of the bathroom. He had rehidden the diamond he still hadn't found the courage to sell, in a tube of toothpaste. If the police found it, he figured with sudden primitive brightness, he would be questioned and perhaps linked up with the Zeller murder; one murder could lead to another and he'd end up in jail.

"In the hall to your left."

Wieland found broom and dustpan.

"What are you going to do?"

"What do you think? What does one usually do with a broom and dustpan. The place looks terrible."

"Doesn't bother me."

"Doesn't it bother your friends?"

"Nobody's been near me since . . . since it happened."

"Nobody?"

"I said nobody. Except for the police, of course. They turned everything upside down."

Wieland began to sweep methodically, under closets, under chests, moving every piece of furniture out of place, back in place. The nephew followed him like a household pet. His bedroom was, if anything, in even worse condition that the other rooms. Here too Wieland found nothing. In the bathroom he seemed interested only in the wastepaper basket, the floor, the bathmat, which he shook vigorously, not in the medicine chest. Heinrich felt faint with relief.

Finally Wieland tackled Mrs. Tummler's bedroom. Why had he left it to the last when, logically, it should have been first? Here the bed had remained unmade, closet door and chest of drawers still stood open as he had seen them after the first search, but in this case the nephew couldn't be blamed. He had been ordered not to touch or move a thing.

Wieland swept under the bed, under the closet, under the chest. The cuckoo popped out of its niche and called softly. "I see you wound the clock."

"Made it seem as if she was still alive, with the bird calling the hours."

Wieland hadn't expected that much sentiment from the man. "Help me turn the mattress."

It was a heavy horsehair mattress. They laid it down

on the floor. Wieland shook the pillows. And suddenly he saw it. The red ribbon of the Legion of Honor. It had been caught at the base of the upholstered headboard. Carefully Wieland pried it loose. It was crumpled and frayed in the middle where a few silk threads were broken. Wieland smiled and pocketed it.

26

Lisa was in tears. "Don't hush me," she told Chris. "Let me cry."

"Then cry darling, if it does you any good."

"Three weeks and three days and I haven't heard from him."

He stroked her hand gently. "It may be impossible for him to write."

"He may be dead."

"I'm sure he's not dead. If he were dead, we'd have heard about it."

"You're sweet." She smiled and put her head on his shoulder. "I don't deserve you."

That was too much. She was so warm; the spot on his shoulder where her head was resting began to burn as if someone had lit a flame there. He drew her closer. Suddenly they were kissing. She didn't seem to notice it, or didn't want to, when he began to undress her, opening her blouse, touching the nipples of her small upright breasts with his lips, pulling down her skirt, stroking the silky insides of her legs. It was a long time since he had felt her flesh react to his hands. Not since she had met Zeller. Since then she had never let him touch her.

Still kissing her, he undressed. She offered no resistance when he entered her. He reached a climax quickly, knew she hadn't. He waited, caressing her, and after a while he took her again. She came, moaning softly, her body arching. But there was a moment when Chris regretted what he enjoyed so much when making love—to see the other's face. It was why he had left the light on on the bedside table. Lisa's face was drawn, her smile was forced. The effort she was making to lead him to believe she had enjoyed him was like a stab of pain. He didn't have to ask why she couldn't be happy; he knew. She would always love the man for whom she had left him. He could understand her so well because in the same way he had betrayed every girl he had slept with since he had lost her. It had always been Lisa.

For a while they lay close, but he made no move to excite her again. She too lay still. After a while she got up and walked through the room and he could hear the shower running. He knew the apartment so well. He found his way to the kitchen in the dark, got out some ice, glasses, scotch. When she came back in a dressing gown, he handed her her drink and went into the bathroom, as he had always done. But when he returned she wasn't lying on the couch as usual. She had disappeared into the bedroom. The door stood ajar. He followed her, lay down beside her, naked, sipped his drink without speaking. She had never liked to talk after making love.

It was very hot in the small room, and he thought— practical as always—tomorrow I'll buy an air conditioner and send it up. He wondered why the idea hadn't occurred to him before, nor to Zeller, for that matter. Without looking at him, Lisa said, "Stay here. Stay through the night."

He stayed. She slept while he lay awake. He knew it would happen again, and that he would always be just a substitute for the man she loved.

27

Wieland had Beaulieu watched. Day and night. Three days after his visit to the clock shop, a call came through to his office. Stieber, one of his men, reported that the red Peugeot had left the garage, driven by a young man with shoulder-length red hair. He had been trailed to a house which he had entered with a large package. He had come out a few minutes later without it. Apparently a delivery. He hadn't gone back to the shop, but had been followed to a badly neglected peasant house above Forch.

Wieland, with a search warrant in his pocket, got into his car and, following Stieber's directions, found the place. Stieber was parked near the house where he could see without being seen. "He's driven off. Report just came in —he drove to the clock shop, picked up another parcel, and left again. Probably another delivery. He's being trailed. Meanwhile I've kept an eye on the house. A hippy commune, judging by the people going in and out."

Near the house sat a young girl, playing a zither. The moment she saw the two men get out of their car, she disappeared. They always made off when they saw strangers. What had turned a whole generation of young people into hunted animals?

There was no bell. They knocked. There was no answer. They walked in. Nobody seemed to be around. A small, untidy kitchen with unwashed dishes on the counters. A living room with bare mattresses spread on the floor, almost covering it. Several other small rooms, equally

149

filthy. Only the last one they entered, near the attic stairs, looked well kept.

Wieland searched it. However often he'd had to do it, poking around in other people's belongings remained distasteful to him. Necessary as it was in his profession, he always felt indiscreet and embarrassed about touching things that didn't belong to him. Because it made him feel guilty, he was all the more conscientious.

There were some clothes in a wardrobe that would have fitted a small man, but they were of cheap material, mostly slacks and turtleneck sweaters. But in one dresser drawer there was expensive underwear, sheer linen. In the corner, a piece of crumpled paper. Wieland took the paper to the window. It turned out to be an old newspaper ad for condominium apartments. It featured a floor plan—the Zeller apartment—in detailed layout.

There was also a box with an amazing assortment of tools. When Wieland asked Stieber to put it on one of the room's two tables and unpack it, the man chose the table covered all the way to the floor with a round, green plastic cloth, fringed. Wieland pushed Stieber aside and lifted the cloth. Under the rickety table stood a small, expensive television set. He jotted down its make and factory number. There was no doubt in his mind that they would coincide with the make and number of the missing Zeller console.

When they returned to the kitchen, a woman was soaking something on the grimy stove. "Are you the owner of the house?"

She nodded. She was elderly, fat, her hair needed washing, and the pupils of her eyes were dilated. Drugs.

"I'd like a list of the people living here," said Wieland, and identified himself.

"Leave me alone," the woman told him. "Every three weeks one of you comes and bothers me. I'm sick of it. My husband died and I keep the place going by taking in boarders. I don't want to sell the place. I've lived here all my life and I'm going to die here. A list? Don't make me laugh. They come and go. Some stay a night, others a couple of days. I ask no questions, which is why they come. How many times have I told all this? I don't want to tell it again. Get out. I'm busy."

150

"Who occupies the room next to the attic stairs?"

She shrugged, ran her fingers through her unkempt hair. "How would I know? They switch around. Sometimes there are three in a room and only one paying rent. Sometimes they're drunk; sometimes they're high on drugs. Go on, arrest them. I couldn't care less. There'll always be more."

"What's the name of the man who occupies the room next to the attic stairs?" Wieland repeated his question, softly.

"You want names? Emilio, Francesco, Herb, Scotty, Gus, Cloud . . . does that help you?"

Gus? "The room near the attic stairs?"

"That's the only decent one. Hardly ever see him. A fag, I'd say. Comes here once in a while, never stays more than a couple of hours. Sometimes lets a friend of his use the room. Pays double when he does. A gentleman."

"Is that Gus?"

"I wouldn't know."

"What does the friend look like?"

"Like all the rest."

"Hair color?"

"Red."

"Long?"

The woman gave him a scathing look.

"All right. Thanks."

28

There was a soft knock on Lisa's door. She looked at the wristwatch Zeller had given her for her last birthday. Nine o'clock.

"Who is it?"

"Gustave. May I come in?"

She opened the door. He came in carrying a bottle of wine. He always brought her a present. "Maybe I should have phoned first, but I heard you walking up and down, up and down, for the last half hour."

"I'm sorry if I disturbed you."

"You didn't disturb me; you worried me." Beaulieu sat down without being asked to stay. "You're restless. I could tell by your steps. And you look upset. Why are you upset?"

"Of course I'm upset," she said. "I can't get Mrs. Tummler out of my mind, lying there as if she were peacefully asleep, and when we moved her head . . ." She shivered.

"You shouldn't have gone there."

"That's beside the point. Why was she murdered? What did she know that somebody had to kill her?"

"Here," said Beaulieu, reaching in his breast pocket and taking out a small pillbox. "Take one of these. It will calm you down."

"What is it?"

"Valium. Ten milligrams. It will quiet you without making you groggy. You can't go on walking up and down all night."

Lisa looked at the pill. It was blue, Valium all right. Beaulieu was right. She should have thought of taking a tranquilizer. She swallowed the pill "There's the girl," said Beaulieu.

Lisa sat down, leaned her head against the back of the chair, closed her eyes. "Wieland thinks she was murdered so she couldn't identify her questioner. What questioner?"

Beaulieu shrugged. "The really important thing she had, we have already."

"You mean the Foley letter?"

"Yes. No trace of him has ever been found. Do you suppose Foley came back? We assume he was after Zeller's findings. Perhaps she knew where they were kept."

She opened her eyes and gave him a look that said quite plainly she found the possibility absurd. "Mrs. *Tummler?*"

Beaulieu shook his head. "Well, no. I guess not. Although she was pretty much the trusted domestic, wasn't she? But I imagine you know more about where he had his files than anyone else. That's probably why they tried you first."

"I guess you're right. It all hangs together." She got up.

"Where are you going?"

"To make myself a cup of coffee. I feel sleepy suddenly, and I don't want to go to bed yet. If I fall asleep now, I'll only wake up a few hours later, and that'll be the end of my night. Shall I make some for you?"

"That's very kind of you."

Beaulieu sipped his coffee slowly. The way he squeezed lemon peel into it made her aware suddenly of his hands. Eyes and hands gave people away, Zeller had said once. "I never know which to look at first. But you can control your eyes to some extent; about your hands, though, you can do nothing." Beaulieu's hands looked cruel. Long palms, short fingers, like claws. Strong hands.

He picked up the conversation where he had left off before she had gone out to the kitchen. "Tell me," he said, "that friend of his, the chemist who was going to analyze and process the vaccine for him . . . couldn't he possibly help us? Zeller might have contacted him. What's his name? Where is he? Let's get in touch with him."

It wasn't a bad idea, she thought, the only thing wrong with it was that it had been tried already. Stadelmann had been in touch with Enrico, who was as distraught as they were and seemed to know even less. He hadn't even had an answer to his letter, written before Helene's death. She was on the point of saying so, when she saw Beaulieu's expression, and it stopped her. He was looking at her, his eyes wide, as if he wanted to hypnotize her. It frightened her. As his hands had done. Why was she suddenly afraid of Beaulieu?

For no reason she could think of, she began to cry. It was all so terrible, so hopeless, and now, so confusing. Beaulieu left his chair and came over to where she half-sat, half-lay on the couch, her legs pulled up under her. "Poor darling," he said. "It must be misery for you."

"Don't." She felt his hand touch her knee and moved away from him. "Please don't. You've been very good to me, Gustave, a real friend. But please don't touch me. It wouldn't work." She almost told him that one of the reasons she had grown fond of him was because he had never tried to make love to her.

He got up and stood looking down at her. Looming over her like that, he seemed much taller, stronger. "Would it comfort you to know where he is?"

It was said so quietly, Lisa couldn't grasp the significance of his words right away. "To know where he is? Of course it would comfort me. What do you mean? You sound as if you know."

"I do," he said. "And I'm ready to strike a bargain with you. Confidence for confidence. I'll tell you where he is if you'll tell me where I can find his files on the vaccine." Again his eyes caught hers in that hypnotic way.

She looked down at her hands, was silent, as the meaning of his words sank in. Then she spoke slowly. "In Stadelmann's office, three weeks ago, you explained that there were certain firms unscrupulous enough to steal what they couldn't buy."

"I did."

"And you are working for such a firm."

"I'm certainly not doing this for myself."

154

"Of course not. You're doing this for money."

Silence.

"You know, of course," she went on, "that Zeller has no intention of letting his vaccine go until he feels it is safe."

"That I have heard *ad nauseam*," said Beaulieu. "Also that he intends to have it processed and manufactured with this friend of his. What I want to know is—does this friend have his findings? And altogether—who is this man?" His smile was the same, but its effect on her now was chillingly different. "But Mrs. Tummler was uncooperative. She refused to give me any information on him, although I know he visited the Zellers frequently. So that left you. I hope you are not going to be as stubborn."

Lisa began to tremble, but knew she had to control herself. "Stubborn? You can't possibly believe that I'm going to reveal anything to you."

"I can't? Not in return for knowledge of where Zeller is?"

"What good would that do me? What good would it do him? He's evidently being kept prisoner somewhere, or he would have contacted Stadelmann."

"And if I can free him?"

She said nothing. This was a different proposition, but she shook it off as equally preposterous. "How can I possibly trust you? Don't be ridiculous."

"I would advise you to trust me. I have been informed that he has not revealed his findings."

"*That* I believe."

"If he continues to refuse, they will kill him."

"Kill him?"

"They could hardly let him go free now, could they? If you tell me where I can find what we're after, you would save his life."

She closed her eyes. He waited patiently for her answer. "I think," she said finally, looking down at her hands again as she spoke, "this is something he will have to decide for himself. Life and death are everyone's own decision, and nobody feels that more strongly than Zeller."

"Perhaps you don't love him anymore."

"What you are asking me to do," she said, "is something that should not be influenced by love."

"By what then?"

"By something you know nothing about. Morality. I have nothing more to say to you."

"We'll see about that. Are you afraid to look at me?"

She looked at him.

"Does his friend have his findings?"

Lisa did not reply.

"Are they in a safe-deposit box somewhere?"

If you were totally truthful, your face betrayed you.

"And you have access to it."

She looked away, closed her eyes. There was something about her stillness that made Beaulieu realize he was not going to succeed, yet he sat with her for almost half an hour. Finally he rose.

"You leave me no choice," he said, and came toward her.

She slipped off the couch and ran from him to the window. She had been taught how to handle psychotics when they became violent, how to resist attack with a minimum of harm to the patient. She did something Beaulieu hadn't expected. She didn't hold up her arms in a vain effort to stop him; she ducked, as he was about to grasp her, and instead of grabbing his legs to make him fall, she let him come at her full force. He sailed over her and hit the sill of the open window just below the hips. She heard his scream, and then the thud with which his body hit the pavement, two floors below.

29

She stood at the window, unable to move, unable to look down at the street. Would she ever get that last sound out of her mind? It was still in her head when Wieland and Graubart broke down her door.

"Why didn't you open?"

"I didn't know it was locked."

"We heard you scream."

Lisa was not aware that she had screamed. "I just killed a man."

"You killed a man?"

"Beaulieu. He was coming at me. Instead of pushing him away . . . I ducked, and let him . . . let him," she could barely speak, "let him fall."

"So it *was* Beaulieu's voice," said Wieland.

Graubart turned on his heels, stopped for a second as a police siren cut through the still of the evening. "My man downstairs must have . . ." He didn't finish his sentence and was gone.

"It is so easy to kill . . . I never knew it was so easy."

"Give me your friend Regina's telephone number."

Lisa could only to point to the desk where her phone book lay.

"Heinz, isn't it? Regina Heinz." He found the number. Dialed.

"I killed Beaulieu," she said again.

"You didn't kill him. You acted in self-defense. That makes all the difference."

"Besides, he isn't dead," said Graubart, coming back into the room. "Badly hurt, yes, but not dead. And now tell us what happened."

"Not now," said Wieland. "Give her time. Tomorrow will do. We've got our man."

"He wanted . . ." She was swaying a little, backward, forward.

Wieland steadied her. "Leave her alone. We know all we have to know."

When Regina came, they left.

30

Two reports from Stieber were waiting for Wieland, one recorded an hour earlier: "He's there"; the second, half an hour later: "Seems to be staying."

Wieland got one of Graubart's men and drove to Forch. Only two windows of the old peasant house showed light, but music from some electronic instruments floated out into the night. Again the front door wasn't locked, and he made his way quietly past the large room, where about ten boys and girls were lying around, sitting, smoking, to the room next to the attic stairs. There was no light showing under the door. He tried the door, found it locked, picked the lock, and entered noiselessly, shading his flashlight beam carefully with his left hand.

A tall fellow, completely naked, lay on top of the bed. A sprinkling of hair showed on his chest. His feet were incredibly dirty and lined with calluses. He seemed fast asleep. Wieland played his flashlight over his face, over the heavy-lidded eyes. The boy sat up and in one movement reached under his pillow and produced a blackjack.

"Put it down," said Wieland, and identified himself.

"What do you want?"

"A few questions. Your name for instance."

"Red."

"Red what?"

"Hunning."

"Registered?"

The boy shrugged.

"You rent this room?"

"Sometimes."

"When?"

"I don't rent it. I don't have that kind of money. A friend lets me sleep here."

"Name of friend?"

"Can't remember."

"Can't remember?"

"C'mon, man . . . one guy helps the other. We don't keep track."

A vicious swing of the blackjack. Wieland evaded it and seized his wrist.

"I advise you not to try that again," he said, and took the weapon from the boy. Suddenly limp, he offered no resistance.

"No money, you say," Wieland continued. "Then how could you afford such an expensive television set?"

"What television set?"

Wieland raised the green plastic tablecover, exposing the set.

"Didn't know it was there."

"That's a lie. You brought it here."

"Well, it doesn't belong to me. Nothing in this room belongs to me."

"It all belongs to your friend whose name you can't remember. Maybe you'll remember in court."

"In court?"

"In court. You're coming along with us."

"I haven't done anything."

"You're harboring stolen goods."

"I didn't steal them.' '

"Then who did?"

"My boss gave them to me."

"Nice present. What did you do for him?"

The boy didn't answer.

"I suppose you don't remember his name either."

"He repairs clocks. I deliver for him."

"And pick up things, don't you? Did you pick up a clock at Helene Zeller's apartment on Krönleinstrasse in July?"

"No. He insisted on going himself."

"Who? Gustave Beaulieu?"

160

"If you know it, why ask me?"

"He's been arrested."

"For what?"

"Murder."

"So what do you need me for?"

"For what you're going to tell us."

While he was getting dressed, Hunning tried to use a knife on Wieland. In the struggle to get it from him, Wieland broke the boy's arm. The boy screamed. The music in the living room stopped. As they passed the door on their way out, Wieland saw that the room was empty. Not a soul. Scattered like nocturnal animals.

31

Zeller was driven to the slaughterhouse blindfolded. As when he had arrived in this country, whose name he still didn't know, a siren shrilled from the top of the car. Once out of the car, led like a blindman by Mercurio, he got an occasional whiff of the sea, the scent of pineapple, and could hear the dry rustle of wind in palm trees. A curtain of eerie silence enveloped him. He suddenly spoke up in Spanish, in an effort to challenge the people around him whom he couldn't see, but could feel watching him. No one replied. In any language.

In the cadaver room, as Mercurio called it, the black scarf was removed. Zeller had come to look upon the young man as a male nurse who came and went according to a doctor's command.

Dr. Grimstone was there to assist. He turned his back discreetly the moment Zeller approached the freshly slaughtered calf. "I don't want you to think we're trying to steal your invention," he told Zeller reassuringly. "All we want you to do is cure our patient." Grimstone's discretion only served to convince Zeller that there were electronic eyes built into the ceiling or walls to do the job for him.

The calf was healthy. Dr. Grimstone had handed Zeller the pathological report before leaving. Written in English. Now Zeller did his best to confuse them. Instead of taking only what he needed, thymus gland and a piece of the aorta, he also removed one kidney, half the lung, and the brain. To his surprise he noticed an open door leading into a lab. It was small, but equipped with all the paraphernalia of a regular hospital laboratory. "How come?" he asked Grimstone.

"You said that speed was of the utmost importance to prevent decomposition of the specimen."

He couldn't remember having said that. It gave him an odd sense of losing his memory. Like very old people who couldn't recall what had happened before, but were able to picture hundreds of events that had taken place in their childhood. His mother, peeling an apple, careful not to break the peel, then throwing it over her left shoulder to see what letter it formed. A person whose first name began with the letter would come to dinner within the week. The extra pocket money he had earned shining his father's shoes or cleaning his medical instruments. The man who had taught his mother how to drive . . . how jealous he had been of him, to the extent of warning his father that there was a strange young man who came, always at four o'clock, and took his mother for a ride. The first maid who had made him sleep with her, coming in while he was in the tub, offering to soap his back, and how magnificent he had felt the next morning. But he couldn't remember having told Grimstone that time was essential in getting the excised organs to the lab.

The lab was disconcerting. He stood in the doorway, taking in the shelves all around three of its walls, a large table, and then he noticed that, as in his room, the door had no handle. What if it fell shut with him inside, left to die, walled in like the condemned in the Middle Ages? He was not afraid of death, but he was determined to die in his own way, to choose the day when he would blow his brains out or walk into the sea and swim until he sank from exhaustion, or take a pill, but always the master of his own existence, even of its end. But to cease living on somebody else's orders? No. He propped the door open with one of the rubber hoses hanging from a hook on the wall.

Dr. Grimstone didn't follow him into the lab. He sat outside on a small uncomfortable stool. Waiting. Zeller decided that there must be a camera, registering every move he made. He used the unnecessary kidney, lung, brains, to make a mash, filling bottles he found standing around. At some time between all this nonsense he did what he had to do. The blenders, American make, whirred. When he finally emerged from the lab, Mercurio was ready with the black scarf.

Back in his room, there was the patient. The man was lying on his stomach on an operating table that had been wheeled in. His head was encased in a nylon stocking. All Zeller was given to see was the man's back, the pajama trousers lowered to below the knees, the shirt pushed up. A good specimen of a body, strong, healthy, much too heavy. He guessed about two hundred and twenty pounds and not quite six feet tall. The skin was smooth, suntanned.

The man spoke no word of greeting, nor did Zeller; he made no sound when Zeller's needle penetrated the gluteus maximus.

Zeller insisted on watching his patient for an hour, but Grimstone said he would supervise the post-treatment care. "Watch for chills," Zeller told him. "Report any abnormalities to me."

Grimstone did, every fifteen minutes. The first time Zeller froze in astonishment when he heard Grimstone's disembodied voice. Then he located the intercom above the handleless door of his room.

32

The days were bad, but the nights were worse. Always Zeller's thoughts reverted to Lisa. It was torture. At times he imagined her so clearly that like a fool, he stretched out his hand to touch her and draw her close. With each day his longing became stronger. He would get up from his bed and sit down at the table to write long letters to her, letters he tore up as soon as he had finished them. It gave him some relief to pretend contact with her on paper, however intangible. He hadn't known how deep his need for her was. In his mind everything about her became exaggerated—her loveliness, her quietude, her devotion, her just being what she was. Mercurio would find the wastepaper basket filled with torn scraps of paper. He didn't say anything, nor did Zeller ask him if he might see a way to get the letters mailed. He knew only too well that Mercurio would have to refuse.

Then there came hours when, hard as he tried, he could not remember her face. All he saw was a blurred outline. He knew this could happen to people who were on the verge of a nervous breakdown. He tried to pull himself together; he couldn't afford to lose his mind. Gradually his memory came back and he could see her clearly again. And the yearning for her grew with every hour. He fought the premonition that he would never see her again. What would happen to him if his patient died? Or lived? There was no answer. There was no answer to any of it.

The days went by. Zeller lost count of them. After the

165

eighth injection, his patient had an adverse reaction. He went into anaphylactic shock. His blood pressure dropped rapidly, his pulse rose to a hundred and sixty. For the first time they didn't wheel the man in; Zeller was taken to his room down a hall. He saw the man's face at last: round, high, prominent cheekbones; a full big mouth; slightly slanting eyes; mongolian features. A face, Zeller believed, that could have been jolly in life, but now, so close to death, it had a solemnity that didn't seem to go with it. He watched the man's profuse perspiration, took his temperature. A hundred and four.

Although Zeller had checked the blood culture report of every animal slaughtered for him, he suspected that the last report had been wrong. His orders had been followed haphazardly, or just insufficiently. The suddenness of this disastrous reaction suggested that the gland he had removed from the calf this morning had contained an infectious agent. That his orders might not have been sufficiently respected infuriated him.

"Cortisone," he told Dr. Grimstone. "One hundred milligrams intravenously, and depending on the patient's response, thirty milligrams every three or four hours, and massive doses of penicillin." He wrote it all down, printing in large clear letters, as if prescribing for morons. Dr. Grimstone looked worried. His immaculate white shirt was crumpled, wet spots showed under the arms. "Is he going to die?"

"I hope not."

Schmidt came in. He usually did, to take a look at his very important patient. He glared at Grimstone, who immediately seemed to know why and said hurriedly, "We had to remove the mask. His condition is critical."

Now Schmidt glared at Zeller. "And what does that mean?"

"Just what you'd think." Zeller's tone was curt. "We either get him through this or we don't."

"Does this mean the treatments can't be continued?"

"Let's take one thing at a time," said Zeller.

He kept his patient on cortisone in reduced dosages for almost two weeks. On the twelfth day he knew that, barring a miracle, the man would die. He told Grimstone, and Grimstone said he had been afraid of this. "I'd appreciate it if *you'd* tell Schmidt." If there had been any capacity left in Zeller for amusement, Grimstone's fear of Schmidt would have struck him as ridiculous.

He told Schmidt.

"If he dies," said Schmidt, "we shall hold you responsible."

Zeller shook his head. Calmly but authoritatively he said, "I am not responsible. You are. You had me kidnapped; you brought me here; you made me go through with this in spite of my warning that the vaccine could be fatal." He didn't mention his suspicion that negligence on their part had given him an impure organ to work with. Let them think the vaccine was at fault. Anything to diminish their opinion of its value.

Zeller was taken back to his room. He found he couldn't concentrate on anything but Schmidt. What kind of a man was he? What had made him what he was today? Revenge on life for the face he had been born with? And who would give him a job, who would have this caricature of a human being around? And his handicap. The crutches. "A gang of older boys stomped me," Schmidt had explained when they had first met. Where? Zeller wondered. Geographically he couldn't place the man. "They broke almost every bone in my body. There wasn't enough money to consult a good doctor, so they knit badly."

Yet he wanted to live. He had risked treatment with an untried vaccine rather than die. Zeller couldn't help but reach the conclusion that Schmidt's desire to live was fed by hatred for everything that was better conditioned, literally, than he. But to practice hatred required power, and power was rooted in money, and Schmidt had found his access to it in a profession, however risky, that was probably one of the most profitable going—industrial espionage. By now Zeller was sure it was the vaccine they were after, no matter how important Schmidt's very sick patient might be.

For whom was Schmidt working? Mercurio, Zeller thought . . . unsure, dependent, cowardly at heart . . . if he could get through to the man, he might be able to find out more about Schmidt. Not that he could see any good it would do him, but the need to know his enemy was almost as strong as the need for freedom, and perhaps even a first step toward extricating himself from his disastrous situation.

Shortly after ten the door to his room opened unexpectedly. Zeller looked up, surprised. He hadn't knocked on the wall to summon Mercurio. Grimstone's last communication over the intercom was to report no substantial change. Was he to be led to his patient's room because he had taken a sudden turn for the worse? But it was Mercurio, and he was holding a finger to his lips to indicate that Zeller shouldn't speak. He walked up to Zeller and whispered in his ear, "Get dressed warmly. Follow me. Along the corridor until you come to a wooden door on your left. It leads to a patio. There'll be another wooden door. If it's locked, climb the wall. It isn't very high. A path leads down to the sea, about five hundred meters. Head for it. I'll meet you in a few minutes."

Was he again doomed to escape into yet another prison?

Zeller did as he was told. As he came out into the open he saw that the building in which he had been kept prisoner was adobe, a whole cluster of buildings actually, with several patios. Bougainvillea climbing the walls. But no flower beds. If his room had had windows, he could easily have escaped on his own, across the tiled roof of the patio that pitched down from the outer wall of the small court, the overhang forming a sort of veranda. Here it was low. He could have jumped to the ground or climbed down a vine. But how far would he have been able to go, not knowing the country or its language?

Behind the buildings, at the end of a wide path, stood a gate, rather pointless since no fences or walls surrounded the property. Beyond it the road was hard-trodden; sugarcane fields on either side. About a hundred yards from the shore, the fields stopped and he was walking on sand. He could see the outline of another building. A sugar mill? He turned right with the road, walked a few steps, thought he heard a sound, and threw himself flat on the ground. He lay there for what seemed a lifetime, his heart beating fast, his throat dry. He could hear the sea lapping at the shore, the cry of a bird, then Mercurio was at his side. "Almost fell over you," he whispered. "Get up. Follow me."

He continued to whisper. "Thank God, for once the weather forecast was correct. Tonight's supposed to be rainy and dark, maybe thunderstorms, which we could do without, but never mind—anything better than a bright moon." He threw Zeller a dark coat. "Put this on."

They walked fast until they came to a stone jetty extending into the sea. Mercurio climbed over it, disappeared, and reappeared in a few minutes, on the water, rowing some kind of a light fishing boat. He brought it up to where Zeller was standing. "Get in. I know what you're thinking, but it's the best I could do. There are no more pleasure craft in Cuba." He pointed toward the distant silhouette of a patrol boat. "We have an outboard motor and a sail on board, but we can't use either until we're past the twelve-mile limit."

Cuba. So that was where they had flown him. And this was obviously another escape. There was much he still had to ask Mercurio, but the man was too busy seating Zeller, settling him with a pair of oars. They were wrapped in burlap. "I hope you're a good rower."

Except for some rowing on Lake Zurich and the Lago Maggiore, Zeller had had little boating experience, and the ocean, with its swell, was a very different proposition from the lakes to which he was accustomed. And the tide was against them. All questioning would have to wait.

It was Mercurio who broke their grim silence. "Well, now it's you and me."

"That's obvious," said Zeller. "You and me for what?"

Mercurio laughed. "Aren't you glad to be rid of that gang?"

"Since I have no idea what gang I'm headed for, I can hardly be glad. Besides, I've left a man behind dying as a result of a treatment for which I had very high hopes. It's hardly the moment for me to be glad."

"Well, I can cheer you up on that score," said Mercurio. "There is nothing wrong with your treatment. That last animal you worked with was poisoned just before slaughtering."

"Poisoned?"

"By me."

"For God's sake, why?"

"Orders."

"Whose orders?"

"You'll find out."

"From my new captors?"

"Well, I can assure you of one thing—they're a better crowd than the ones we left behind."

"Since I don't know whom I left behind, I won't be able to see much improvement, will I? Don't you think you'd better clear me up?"

"It's a long story," said Mercurio, "and you'll agree that this isn't exactly the time for it. Our friends are going to meet us just as soon as we get out of territorial waters. Curb your curiosity until then, and row, man, row!"

33

As predicted, the weather changed. A few stars had shown up timidly in the sky, and Zeller had made out an enormous *cumulonimbus,* with a well-defined anvil on top, directly above them. Mercurio had cursed the possibility that there might yet be moonlight, then the storm had broken, whipping the sea, which until then had merely rolled a bit, into waves that broke over them, soaking them through and accumulating water in the bilge. The boat spun around. "Row!" Mercurio shouted, "and steer."

They managed to straighten the boat, but the next wave nearly capsized them. It took with it the outboard motor resting in the stern, the food stored under one of the thwarts, and the pails. "Bail!" shouted Mercurio. "I know the pails are gone. Use your hands!"

The storm abated. "And we weren't swept out." Mercurio grimaced. "The sharks here are ferocious." He reached into his pocket, pulled out a compass. "Thank God, I still have it. I thought I'd put it down next to me." He looked at it, then put it back into his pocket carefully. "All right," he said. "We're on course."

"Where are we heading?"

"Florida, where else?"

"I don't have a passport."

"You have a passport, Mr. Gumprecht. A perfectly good passport's waiting for you."

Perhaps the most absurd part of it all was that the

only thing Zeller could think of to say was, "What a dreadful name!"

Mercurio turned around, grinning. The crazy nut seemed to be enjoying it all! "Can't be choosy about things like that," he said. "A Mr. Gumprecht just happened not to need his passport anymore."

Zeller wondered if Mr. Gumprecht's need of a passport had ended naturally or involuntarily, but he didn't ask. At this point he didn't want to know any more.

"Let's hoist the sail," said Mercurio, "if it's still there."

It was. The wind caught it, and it billowed like a black cloud over their heads. It was the first black sail Zeller had ever seen. Made for their escape, he imagined.

Hours later, as dawn began, Mercurio let out a sigh of unmistakable relief. "We're out of territorial waters," he said. He was trying to light a flare. The first two were too wet to go off. "I've only got one more," he said, "God help us." It sounded like a prayer.

It went off. A while later, the sun at their backs, they spotted a boat coming rapidly closer. A pleasure yacht, well over fifty feet. It was flying the American flag. "Thank God!" Mercurio stood up, waving both arms. "They had to keep moving, or the patrol boats would have gotten suspicious. Others trying to escape have been met by yachts. I timed it all right, didn't I?" He was obviously proud of himself and much too relieved not to show it.

When they were close enough to the yacht, someone on board threw a line. Neither of them was able to catch it, so it was pulled in and thrown out again. Zeller caught it this time, and they were drawn close. Mercurio, his hands fending them along the side of the boat, maneuvered them to a rope ladder. Zeller almost lost his footing on the wet rungs. Hands reached out and pulled him aboard, after him, Mercurio.

A large afterdeck, open in good weather, but enclosed now by a clear plastic canopy. Rattan furniture, a vinyl couch, a few small tables, fixed to the deck. A radio, not turned on. An illuminated instrument panel. A steward in white, with a slicker over his shoulders. Scotch and glasses on a tray. "Or would the gentlemen prefer brandy?"

"Brandy," Zeller told the man. "And if possible, hot tea."

172

The brandy was instantly forthcoming, the hot tea arrived soon after, together with a platter of open sandwiches—roast beef, smoked salmon, cheese. Zeller discovered he was ravenous. And then—a man. In his early forties. Tall, slim, square-jawed, crewcut. "Holstein," he introduced himself. "Glad to have you on board," and to Mercurio, "You did a good job, Foley."

Foley? Zeller saw an angry frown pass across Mercurio's face. "I thought we'd decided to bury Foley," he said sharply.

Holstein was smiling, not a pleasant smile. "As it turned out," he said, "we've had to resurrect him again." He turned to Zeller. "I am honored to meet you, Professor Zeller."

So at least he was still running under his own name.

The man had a tic under his left eye. A sign of nervousness? Possibly. He should do something about it, thought Zeller. It was strong enough to pull up the right side of his mouth for the split second it took to reveal false teeth.

"Yes, you did a good job," Holstein told Mercurio a second time.

Mercurio shrugged. "Why not? Your orders were explicit; your contacts came through. Everything worked out on schedule."

"What schedule?" asked Zeller.

Holstein seemed ready to explain. He leaned back in his chair, his lips parted to speak, but just as Zeller felt that his curiosity was at last to be satisfied, Holstein shook his head. "Tomorrow," he said. "We'll talk after you've had a good rest."

He pressed a bell. A husky man appeared, not tall but obviously strong, with a short black mustache, dressed like a steward, all in white.

"This is Nero," Holstein introduced him. "Don't be reminded of the Roman emperor. He doesn't go in for setting fires. He's got other idiosyncrasies." He laughed at his own joke and Nero smiled broadly. Mercurio/Foley saw nothing to laugh at.

The three of them followed Nero through a salon. A few steps down they proceeded past a galley into a narrow passageway off which several doors opened. They were ushered into a cabin with two beds.

"Is there a shower?" asked Mercurio, and regardless of everyone, he began to undress.

"Of course," said Holstein. "I'm sorry I didn't think before of how waterlogged you must be. And now, if you'll excuse me, I'll go up to the bridge and talk to my captain. If there's anything you want, gentlemen, Nero will be at your disposal. I hope you'll sleep long and well. See you tomorrow. As late as you like."

Zeller, too exhausted to take a shower, threw off his clinging clothes and crawled into bed. "I've been fighting off sleep," he said, when Mercurio emerged from the bathroom, "because I'm confused. Why the hell does Holstein call you Foley?"

"That's my business."

"Not a very pleasant business—at least that's the impression you gave."

No reply.

"So what am I supposed to call you?"

"Call me anything you damn please," said Mercurio/Foley, turning his back and pulling the bedcovers up to his ears.

34

It was afternoon when Zeller woke up. His suit, dry and neatly pressed, hung over a clothes valet next to his bed. After a while he realized that the rumble of the engines had stopped. He looked at Foley, who was still fast asleep. Zeller got up, dressed, found the salon. Nero was there.

"Would you like something to eat?" he asked pleasantly.

Zeller ordered and downed an enormous meal, determined not to allow himself to think until he knew more. Odysseus, he remembered, stopped up his crew's ears so they could not hear the song of the Sirens. Everything he had experienced since they had got him out of jail, and before that, was too fantastic to understand.

"When you are finished," said Nero, "Mr. Holstein would like to see you. You are please not to hurry."

Zeller didn't. He could wait. He smoked a cigarette. Then, guided by Nero, he found Mr. Holstein in a swivel chair on the lower deck, a fishing rod clamped between his knees. In his left hand he was holding a drink—a bullshot.

"Absolutely addicted to deep-sea fishing," he said. "Want to try?"

"Not interested at all."

"Thought so. But it's an exciting sport. The fight to bring in a sailfish . . . pity they aren't running now. Got one over four feet long last season. A beaut. Had it stuffed and mounted. Hangs in my office. But the kings will have to do."

"Where are we heading?"

"Florida. I plan to land in the late evening."

"Mercurio tells me I have a passport."

"Foley," Holstein corrected him. "Yes, you have a passport. Everything taken care of. You have nothing to worry about."

His teeth clicked slightly when he spoke. In spite of his apparent wealth—if he was the owner of this yacht—he must have had a poor dentist. Zeller wondered if he took his teeth out before he made love to a woman. And this is the sort of thing you think, he told himself, when you're running scared.

"And still," said Zeller, "I am worried. I'm not accustomed to entering a foreign country under an assumed name, with a passport that isn't mine. If you don't mind, I'd like to ask a few questions."

"Not at all," said Holstein, and put away his equipment. He took a soft leather case from his breast pocket. It held three cigars. "Havanas." He offered Zeller one. Zeller declined.

"Who are you?"

Holstein lit his cigar carefully. "So you want me to put my cards on the table."

"If you will, please."

"Well then—who am I? I am an employee of a chemical concern. In that capacity I am under contract to deliver your findings, which will make it possible for our firm to duplicate and manufacture your vaccine. When we heard that you were refusing to sell it, we tried to . . . shall we say obtain it by other means? But we failed, although we had one of our best men working on it."

"Foley?"

Holstein's smile was contemptuous, but all he said was, "No."

"All right," said Zeller. "But as you undoubtedly know, I was abducted to Cuba to treat a very sick Cuban."

"What makes you think he was Cuban?" Holstein's teeth made that exasperating noise again as he got them back into position.

"I took it for granted."

"That," said Holstein, "is something one should never do."

176

"So what nationality was he?"

Holstein raised his shoulders and opened his eyes wide in an expression of mock innocence.

"He had Mongolian features. I'll admit, he certainly didn't look like a Latin. Was he Russian?"

This brought Holstein back to speech. "My dear Herr Professor," he said. "You are so immersed in medicine and in your specific and—if I may say so—spectacular application to research, that perhaps you don't go as deeply into politics as men like myself have to. In this nuclear age, the great powers try to carry on their . . . shall we say slightly underhand dealings as much as possible outside their own countries. But all this is none of our concern."

"I consider it my concern," said Zeller. "My patient is going to die."

"Is already dead," said Holstein. "He died this morning, at 8:05, while you were asleep."

"How do you know?"

"How do you think? How do you think your escape was initiated? We have our collaborators in Cuba. We have them wherever we need them."

"The man was murdered."

"That's right. Though I must admit, it was not part of the original plan. The security on you was a bit more elaborate than we had bargained on. We had to go beyond our . . . collaborators, to a certain political element on the island, in order to effect your escape. The man's death was, shall we say, our half of the bargain."

"And you tell me this . . . I know it must sound idiotic to you, but I'll say the word just the same . . . shamelessly?"

"I would have cause for shame only if you were not here with us now. Has it occurred to you yet, Herr Professor, how extremely well it suited us that we didn't have to shoulder the responsibility of removing you from jail? Schmidt did us a great favor. It is going to make things very much simpler for us."

Holstein's smile, Zeller decided, was the most unpleasant one he had ever come across. The man should never smile.

Schmidt never had. Somehow the two men, however different in appearance, merged in his mind.

"You had to be told," said Holstein. "We can't have you thinking your vaccine is unsafe. In our opinion it is not. In our opinion it is far enough advanced, in fact much farther advanced, than some products we have bought. We hope you will see it our way."

"I am not going to see it your way," said Zeller.

"We are ready to pay for the rights. Pay well. It will be patented under your name, jointly with ours. Our team of chemists is one of the finest in the world. You will head the project, on a substantial salary. Or if you prefer to go back to your surgical work, we will be glad to give your Italian friend the job of supervision. We *would* like to know what you have been offered by other firms. We are ready to pay you considerably more."

"I don't want your money."

His answer seemed to astonish Holstein. "I don't believe it. You know, there are very few people who would turn down such a fortune."

"Well, I am one of them."

"We intend to be the first to manufacture your vaccine," said Holstein, lighting a fresh cigar, although he had smoked the first one only halfway down. Suddenly Zeller had to laugh. "What is amusing you?" asked Holstein.

"I was thinking . . . you know so much, yet you seem unaware of the fact that your offer couldn't work. Have you forgotten that I am under suspicion of murdering my wife? Or were you planning to do all this with me posing as Mr. Gumprecht?"

"Of course not," said Holstein, in a tone that was almost soothing. "The Gumprecht passport is a safeguard. We will probably never have to use it. Because, if you agree to our plan, as I am sure you will, you will be Professor Zeller, no one else, who was kidnapped by Russian agent Ilya Komarov, alias Smith and other names . . . you see, as I already said, how this little Cuban interlude suited us. And it was our man in Zurich who made that clear to me. A genius. But . . . back to you. So, we arranged your escape. We return you to the authorities in Zurich . . ." he paused.

"And I go back to jail. Mr. Holstein, you don't make sense."

"I don't? That you go back to jail was your conclusion, not mine. You see, I happen to know who killed your wife, and what is more—I can produce the man. So I am ready to offer you the following deal: I hand over the man to the authorities in return for the vaccine. You return to Switzerland to clear yourself, and we have a contract with you."

Zeller was too stunned to speak. The whole incredible plan took time to filter through the confusion in his mind, ending up always at the point that he would be free, free to work, to live the way he wanted, free to marry Lisa. But the plan was too neat; there had to be a hitch somewhere.

"But how can you possibly know who killed Helene?"

"I do."

"One of your men?"

"When you have signed the contract."

"And if I decide that even for the price of liberty I couldn't possibly . . ."

"You needn't decide anything now," Holstein interrupted him. "I understand your reluctance, and I'm a considerate man. I'll give you four days to think it over. I want us to get to know each other. So . . . would you like a drink?"

"Nothing right now," said Zeller.

For the next hours, they sat around talking about nothing in particular. Impossible even to concentrate on that. It was dark when they entered the south inlet of Lake Worth.

"It's not easy," Holstein told Zeller, "to get in here without mishap. From smaller boats people have fallen overboard and drowned. The tide in this narrow inlet is extremely dangerous." There was a glint in his eyes.

"You seem to enjoy danger."

Holstein nodded. "The salt of life."

Zeller looked up at the circular bridge. It was, he thought, a quite beautiful structure. As if he could read his thoughts, Holstein said, "They may take it down."

They made fast at a reserved slip on a concrete jetty. A moment later Zeller stood on American territory. A

179

car was waiting for them. As they got in, Holstein said, "Your four days of reflection begin as of now."

It was Thursday evening. The time, ten minutes after ten.

35

Holstein's house lay behind high ixora hedges, completely hidden from the road. Even from the sea, the low, narrow building was barely visible, with dunes artificially built up in front of it. The stretch of beach was fenced on both sides. On one side stood a blue-and-white painted cabana with a shower and a bar, and it was here that Holstein spent most of his time, phoning or listening to the radio, with Nero in steady attendance.

Two days had gone by since Zeller had landed on American soil, pleasant days. Lots of sleep, decent food, and the sun, uninterruptedly. He was tanned, as if after a long vacation. Without having to do anything about it himself, he had been issued appropriate clothes, of much finer style and more expensive than had been handed out to him in Cuba. The only thing that was lacking—and this seemed to be the crazy pattern of his life now—was freedom.

The stretch of beach on which he and Foley were sunning was glaringly white. In the shade of the cabana sat Nero. Two Dobermans, their black coats glistening in the sun, were tied to a boat with an outboard motor beached a few feet up on shore. The dogs' long leashes gave them just enough leeway to get a yard or two into the water to cool off. Sleekly groomed, deadly animals. The ocean seemed to stretch to an infinite horizon ahead of them. Behind them lay the house. A terrace, half-glass enclosed, half-covered by a bright orange awning, faced the beach. Their room, overlooking the beach, was located off it. There were no bars on its window. Who needed bars with the two Dobermans?

Zeller had come to no decision. The problem was insoluble. He thought of Lisa and decided to accept; he thought of having to give up the plans he had made for the vaccine, the loss of independence and integrity inherent in Holstein's offer, and decided no. And these vacillations sometimes repeated themselves within minutes.

"How long have you known Holstein?" Zeller asked.

He had grown almost fond of Foley, who gave the impression that he simply couldn't help being what he was. The fact that he seemed perpetually tense since their arrival in Florida had perhaps caused this sudden empathy.

"Never saw him before he picked us up."

"Then how could you work for him?"

"Middlemen," said Foley, and when Zeller said nothing, "sometimes I envy you for not knowing what goes on in our world."

"Why stay in it when you seem to hate it?"

"Caught," said Foley. "The money was irresistible."

"And the adventure?"

"Could be. If you want to analyze it. When I think about it, I never get much beyond my own financial desperation . . . well no, that's not exactly fair. I wasn't really poor, but the things I wanted, the good life . . . oh yes, of course I mean materially . . . that's light years away."

"The dishonesty never bothered you?"

"With what we see going on all around us? Are you serious? I don't believe—and I say this sincerely—that there is anyone around these days who has made big money . . . I don't mean now inherited money . . . but who had made big money in his own lifetime and been scrupulously honest. At least I work for what I earn, and with great danger to my life, but they're the ones who make a pile out of it. So that part of it at least is honest."

Zeller had to smile at the convoluted rationale by which Foley had arrived at this honesty.

"And now you're holding us up," Foley went on, his eyes closed, his voice angry, "because Holstein says he
182

won't pay me until you've said yes. The job, he says, isn't over until then. And I want that money. I'm getting out of this racket. I've had it."

"I have two days left," said Zeller, "and I need them."

Foley's laugh was derisive. "Why do you need two more days? All you have to do is sell your almighty cure to Holstein and you have nothing more to worry about. Whereas if you don't . . ."

"Exactly. What if I don't?"

"Then I'm afraid Mr. Gumprecht would fall overboard from a pleasure yacht, and drown."

"Oddly enough," said Zeller, "that's a possibility I haven't given much thought to. What worries me are things you couldn't possibly understand. But I have been relieved of one worry, or I think I have. As you know, I'm wanted in Zurich for the murder of my wife. But Holstein tells me he knows who murdered her, and he's ready to deliver the man in exchange for a contract signing over my vaccine, which certainly changes the picture. In a sense. But how can I be sure that he really knows who murdered my wife? How could he know?"

He was so absorbed with what he was saying, more to himself than to Foley, that he didn't notice how the latter froze, his eyes open wide now, unblinking. Into the silence, Foley said, "Holstein knows who murdered your wife?"

"That's what he says."

Another silence, then Foley said, "Well, it's a tempting offer."

"Tempting, yes. Right now I think I'm going to accept; five minutes from now, I'll change my mind."

And that's the thread by which I'm hanging, thought Foley, but all he said was, "Count it off on a daisy," in a tone that surprised Zeller with its harshness. Then he got up. "I'm going in for a swim," he said, and was gone, without asking Zeller to join him.

Foley swam far out. If only he could make it to one of the adjacent beaches. But there was Nero, getting into the boat. There was no escape.

He turned and floated on his back, the whole disastrous business unfolding in his mind. The news of Helene's letter, found by the housekeeper and implicating him, had come over the air on their flight to Cuba. And Cuba had seemed a haven. Not that he had expected any protection from Smith, but he would have been paid and could have disappeared. The alliance with Holstein, via Beaulieu, and the escape from the island, had merely postponed all that, but then Holstein had resurrected "Foley" and now, from what Zeller had said, he again had cause for alarm.

He started to swim back. He didn't see the white beach drawing nearer: he saw Helene, opening the door to the library, he saw her frightened expression when, expecting only her lover, she had seen two men. Why had she suddenly appeared? To talk to him? Perhaps to stop him from going through with it? Or had she just been aroused by Beaulieu's voice, rising with impatience when, among the papers in the safe—securities mostly—they had found nothing that resembled a medical data file. She had gasped. Before she could say or do anything, Beaulieu had turned, slammed one hand over her mouth, and simultaneously hit hard with the side of his other hand against the back of her neck. Helene sank to the floor. Beaulieu picked up her motionless body and carried her into the bedroom. He came out again a few minutes later, smiling. "What did you do to her? You didn't kill her?" And Beaulieu, "Idiot! I just put her out while we finish up here," and then nothing but silence, no sound from the bedroom. He had wanted to look; Beaulieu hadn't let him . . .

Dwelling on what Zeller had told him, Foley recalled Holstein's remark after he had advised him of the murder: "That's unfortunate. Beaulieu is not expendable."

No, but he, Graham Foley, was. He saw the game now. Clearly, Holstein intended to expose him as the murderer in exchange for the Zeller contract. And there was the letter to corroborate it. How in God's name could he ever prove his innocence?

36

The conversation with Foley on the beach that morning had added a new possibility to Zeller's quandary. What *would* happen to him if he said no? The realization hit him full force: he had to count on the probability of his own death. One thing, though, became increasingly clear—if he ever got out of this maze, he would have his vaccine analyzed, patented, tested, and, in due course, marketed. There was no alternative. He could not go on as a prey to unscrupulous drug racketeers.

He was getting ready to undress when Foley, sitting in a chair, staring intently into space, said, "There's something I have to tell you. Something you don't know. You are under suspicion of having murdered your wife, true, but so am I."

"You?"

It would never have occurred to Zeller that Foley was capable of killing anyone. He wasn't even cut out for the job he'd undertaken.

"But I didn't do it," Foley went on. "Beaulieu did."

"Beaulieu? Who is Beaulieu?"

"Holstein's man in Zurich. Gustave Beaulieu. A repairer of antique clocks. At least that's his present cover. But Holstein intends to pin the murder on me. I've got to get out of here if I'm ever to prove my innocence. Will you help me? If I'm successful, you'll be free too."

Zeller took his time answering. Foley was staring at him anxiously.

"I'm going to try to reach the police," Foley went on.

"How?"

"I'll try to make it to the boat. It's the only possibility I can see. But you've got to distract their attention and hold them off until I can get started. You get out first through the bathroom window, I'll wait and get out here," he pointed to the bedroom window facing the beach, "just as soon as I hear the dogs."

Zeller pondered the idea for a moment, then he said, "It could work." And after a pause, "When?"

"Now."

Zeller went to the bathroom. The window was small. He pushed out the screen and managed to squeeze through. He hadn't progressed more than thirty yards when the dogs rushed him, barking furiously. And there was Nero, gun drawn.

"Where do you think you're going?"

"For a walk. Alone. The walls were caving in on me."

"How did you get out?"

Zeller pointed. "Through the bathroom window. For God's sake leash those animals." The dogs were still snarling around his legs.

Nero gave a sharp command. They sat down quivering. He shoved Zeller toward the front of the house. Zeller pretended to stumble, and fell. Nero helped him up. Zeller groaned.

"What's the matter?"

Zeller was standing on one leg; gingerly he tried to put down the other foot, winced. "It's my ankle. I guess I've sprained it. You shouldn't shove people around like that. This gravel's slippery. Damn it, you're going to have to help me in."

He slung his arm around Nero's shoulders. He would have liked to strangle the man, but with the dogs . . . and then Holstein was standing at the front entrance. "You fool," he said to Zeller, putting his revolver away, and to Nero, "Take him back to his room."

Holstein followed them in. First Nero, then Holstein stared at the empty beds, then around the room. "Where's Foley?"

Zeller shrugged. "Where should he be? In the bathroom."

When would he hear the motor? He tried to calm himself with the thought that in front of the house, with the dogs barking, he had perhaps not heard it. Or had he given Foley too little time? And then it came, sputtering, but loud and clear.

Holstein and Nero looked at each other, their mouths set. "He's gone to call the police," Zeller told them.

Nero drew his gun. "Don't," said Holstein. He gestured with his head in the direction of the door, and suddenly both of them were gone, their hurried steps receding. Zeller stood still, too stunned to move, expecting them back any moment. Not until he heard the car starting, revving up, and tearing into the night, did he realize that they were not returning.

Slowly he walked through the quiet house. It was all his. The front door was open. He stood in the doorway, looking out across the beautifully tended tropical garden, palm trees silhouetted against a sky that was brightening as the moon rose higher, a picture-postcard setting. It seemed to him that he had been standing there only a short while when he heard the sound of a police siren.

37

A knock at her door, and when Lisa opened it, there was Stadelmann, wiping perspiration from his round face, as though he had run up the stairs without once stopping for breath. For just a second Lisa drew back, alarmed, then sense told her that nobody, least of all Stadelmann, would hurry up two flights of stairs to bring bad news.

She paled. "You heard from him?"

He nodded. "American police called from Florida. He's all right. Nothing to worry about, not any longer. Sorry to be so short, but I have to catch the plane. Your phone must be out of order, that's why I stopped by to let you know. Got a taxi waiting downstairs."

He turned. Lisa ran down after him. "You talked to him?"

Stadelmann shook his head. "Just to the police."

"Why didn't he call me?"

"Maybe they wouldn't allow him to contact anyone . . ." He was already climbing into the car.

"Wait—I'll drive with you to Kloten."

"In a nightgown?" Stadelmann yelled back and was gone. Lisa looked down at herself. It was true. There she stood on the street in a short, sleeveless dressing gown and slippers. Up in her room she threw herself back onto her bed. He was alive! He was safe! Nothing to worry about, Stadelmann had said. Nothing to worry about any longer. Relief and happiness made her cry. After a while she dialed Wieland's number. The line was dead, then she remembered Stadelmann telling her that her phone was out of order. She cursed, got dressed, and walked to the nearest telephone booth.

"Yes, I know," said Wieland. "And I'm happy for you and him, but it will take a little time to clear everything up. You must be patient now. No, no. There won't be any difficulties. If everything works out all right, the case against him will be dismissed. Just be happy and patient."

Days went by, each slower and longer than the preceding one. Lisa refused to leave her room for fear Zeller might call and she'd miss him. Wieland came up to explain the red tape and formalities it took to confirm the whole fantastic story Zeller was telling, the endless cables, telephone calls, questions and answers going back and forth so that Zeller could enter his native country as a free man. "Zbinden is behaving very well, indeed. No attempt on his part to create difficulties."

Chris came to offer congratulations, a bit morosely.

Regina managed to take three days off to help Lisa pass the time. "I've never seen you so emotional."

"I had to hold on to myself, or I would have gone crazy, but now . . ."

"You'd better take a grip of yourself," Regina warned. "After what he apparently went through he might be a changed man."

His call came finally, in the middle of the night.

"*Salut,*" Zeller said.

His voice hadn't changed. It was strong and, as always when he was deeply moved, drier than usual.

"*Salut,*" Lisa answered, as if it were yesterday that they had last talked to each other.

"I want you to meet me in Milan," Zeller told her. "Day after tomorrow. At Enrico's."

"At Enrico's?"

"I've got to talk to him as soon as possible. Call him right away, will you? Please. Tell him he won't have to wait any longer. Besides, I don't want us to get caught with the press when the story breaks. Can you hear me all right? Or do you want me to ask for another line? Your voice sounds so small."

"I can hear you all right."

"Day after tomorrow, then."

"It seems a terribly long time."

"So it does," said Zeller.

THE ELECTRIFYING TRUE STORY
OF THE MOST DARING MANHUNT
OF OUR TIME!

After-
math

Ladislas Farago

Bestselling Author of
THE GAME OF THE FOXES and PATTON

The *true* story of Ladislas Farago's courageous and relentless search for the Führer's right-hand-man and confidant, Martin Bormann . . . and how he finally came face-to-face with the most wanted Nazi war criminal of all!

**A REAL-LIFE SAGA OF SUSPENSE
AND INTERNATIONAL INTRIGUE**

"THE STUFF OF WHICH THRILLERS ARE MADE."
Los Angeles Times

25387 / $1.95

Available wherever paperbacks are sold, or directly from the publisher. Include 25¢ per copy for mailing; allow three weeks for delivery. Avon Books, Mail Order Dept., 250 West 55th Street, New York, N.Y. 10019.   AF 8-75

AVON ◆ 24299
$1.75

THE HEART-STOPPING,
HEARTBREAKING NOVEL
OF FOUR HUMAN BEINGS
CAUGHT IN A DEATH-STRUGGLE
FOR LIVES AND NATIONS!

ENDGAME

THE STUNNING
INTERNATIONAL BLOCKBUSTER
By HARVEY ARDMAN

As the superpowers bargain for Arab oil and
Israeli loyalty, three men and a woman battle
for possession of a secret nuclear device
which threatens millions of lives. Hurtling
across Europe to the Mid-East inferno, END-
GAME is the electrifying saga of passion,
treachery, counterespionage, and human des-
tiny—as shattering as today's headlines!

Now an Avon paperback on sale
everywhere, or order direct from the
publisher. Address Avon Books, Mail
Order Department, 250 West 55th St.,
New York, N.Y. 10019. Include 25¢ per
copy for mailing; allow three weeks
for delivery.

EN6-75